He was a hero.

He stood there, a smile lighting his eyes, looking so proud of himself. As proud as she was that he'd rescued his niece and her kittens from the tree. But wasn't that what firefighters always did?

"Uncle Liam needs a hug."

His niece's statement broke into her thoughts. She looked at the girl, who wore the biggest grin. Did she want Sarah to hug him? Then again, hadn't he just saved one of her precious pets? Heat suffusing her face, she gave him a quick embrace.

She led him out of the yard, Liam following close behind her. She kept her head forward, her cheeks still flaming. At the gate, she swiveled around. "I shouldn't have done that."

He closed the space between them. "I'm glad you did. I can always use a hug. It's been a difficult time adjusting to fatherhood, and I have a feeling it's been hard for you, too, since you came back home."

Yes, it was. And as she looked at Liam, she had a feeling it was going to get even harder…

Margaret Daley, an award-winning author of ninety books, has been married for over forty years and is a firm believer in romance and love. When she isn't traveling, she's writing love stories, often with a suspense thread, and corralling her three cats that think they rule her household. To find out more about Margaret, visit her website at margaretdaley.com.

Books by Margaret Daley

Love Inspired

The Firefighter Daddy

Lone Star Cowboy League

A Baby for the Rancher

Caring Canines

Healing Hearts
Her Holiday Hero
Her Hometown Hero
The Nanny's New Family

A Town Called Hope

His Holiday Family
A Love Rekindled
A Mom's New Start

Helping Hands Homeschooling

Love Lessons
Heart of a Cowboy
A Daughter for Christmas

Visit the Author Profile page at Harlequin.com for more titles.

The Firefighter Daddy

Margaret Daley

Recycling programs
for this product may
not exist in your area.

 LOVE INSPIRED BOOKS

ISBN-13: 978-0-373-81901-0

The Firefighter Daddy

Copyright © 2016 by Margaret Daley

www.Harlequin.com

Printed in U.S.A.

For the Lord is good;
His mercy everlasting,
And His truth endures to all generations.
—*Psalms* 100:5

To all firefighters, you do a great job.
Thank you.

Chapter One

The sound of a loud crash from the rear of the shop reverberated through Snip and Cut Hair Salon. Sarah Blackburn held her scissors poised over her customer's white hair for a second then whirled around and looked at her mother in the station next to hers. She was in the middle of shampooing a client. "I'll take care of it, Mom. Mrs. Calhoun, I'll be right back."

Sarah made a beeline for the small kitchen area, her heart pounding. What had Nana done now? Please, God, let her be okay.

Sarah entered the room and came to a sudden halt. Nana stood in the middle of a puddle of red and brown dyes splattered all over the tiled floor with a large cat racing through the color mixture toward the open bay window. The tomcat, with splashes of red and brown on its white fur, leaped onto the table, jumped to the windowsill and wiggled his big body under the raised screen, disappearing from sight.

"Oh, dear. Sammy didn't even finish his food." Her forehead knitted, Nana glanced at Sarah. "I need to find him."

Before her grandmother started for the rear door, Sarah moved into action, cutting off her path. She slung her arm around Nana's thin shoulders and turned her away. "You've got dye on your legs. I need to scrub it off before it turns your skin red and brown." She sat her grandmother in the chair nearby, grabbed a wet cloth and began scrubbing the dye off her skin.

"Sammy will get hungry if I don't go get him."

"Nana, the tomcat is long gone. How did you get him inside? He usually eats outside on the back stoop."

"I left the door open while I fixed his food. He came in." Nana beamed. "Until lately, Sammy hasn't always come to me."

"Sammy," as her grandmother called the white tomcat that had been showing up lately at the shop, was a stray that Nana thought was her pet when she was a little girl.

"Mama, what did you do?" Sarah's mother asked as she charged into the kitchen.

Nana peered at her daughter and pursed her

lips. "My job. I was preparing a dye for a customer. One bowl slipped from my hand, and I must have dropped the other. The sound scared Sammy. I've got to find him."

Sarah's mom sighed, her shoulders drooping forward as she faced Sarah. "Go finish Mrs. Calhoun's cut then style Beatrice's hair for me. I'm taking her home—" she glanced at Nana "—and get her cleaned up. Good thing they're our last clients."

As her mom took over with Nana, Sarah reentered the front of the small hair salon, plastering a grin on her face, when she didn't feel like smiling. Not when she understood her grandmother's need to look for what she thought was her pet. Three days ago Sarah's dog had disappeared. A lump lodged in her throat at the thought of not seeing Gabe again. Her late husband had given her the black Lab on their second anniversary, and Gabe had helped her get through the deaths of Peter and her unborn child. Many late nights she'd held the Lab and cried over her loss.

"Is everything okay?" Mrs. Calhoun's question drew Sarah from the past, and she mentally shook Peter from her thoughts.

"Nana dropped a bowl of dye. No big deal. Mom is taking care of her." Sarah shifted toward Mrs. Miller, who was sitting in her mother's booth with wet hair. "I'll be with you soon. Mom had to drive Nana home."

Beatrice Miller snorted, muttering, "I told your mother Carla needed to be put in a nursing home."

Sarah took a deep breath and refrained from saying anything to the woman who wasn't that many years away from retirement herself. She hurried to her customer, snatching up her scissors. "I only have to make sure it's even, Mrs. Calhoun, then blow-dry your hair and—"

"Nonsense. It's almost dry, and I love this short cut the way it is. You have more pressing issues to take care of, dear." The older woman winked at Sarah in the mirror and gave her a huge grin as she turned and pointedly looked at Mrs. Miller.

It was people like Mrs. Calhoun that had made it bearable coming home to Buffalo, Oklahoma, after fleeing five years ago because of the overwhelming memories of what she'd lost, crushing her until she hadn't even wanted to leave her house.

It was the thought of Mrs. Calhoun's smile and wink, which Sarah carried with her through fixing Mrs. Miller's hair and listening to the woman's complaints the whole time she did, that helped. After she left the shop, Sarah cleaned up the mess in the kitchen, locked up then slid behind the steering wheel of the re-stored yellow MINI Cooper that Peter had given her on their first anniversary.

As she headed to her mom's house, she glimpsed a sign for the highway that led to Tulsa, and the urge to go there swamped her. Only home three months, she felt as though she were experiencing the loss of Peter all over again everywhere she went in Buffalo. She hadn't even been able to drive by the house they had rented and had been thankful it wasn't near any of the usual places she frequented.

She approached the intersection where an old man had run a stop sign and changed her life forever. Forcing herself to continue, since it was the fastest way home, she crept toward it, her hands shaking. Usually she avoided it. She tightened her grip on the steering wheel and kept going at ten miles under the speed limit.

Out of the corner of her eye she caught a glimpse of a poster on a telephone pole of a black Lab. She pulled over to the curb, forti-fied herself with a deep breath, climbed from her car and then jogged over to the picture to read it.

One look at the black Lab on the sign and she knew it was Gabe. Her spirits soared at the prospects of getting her dog back. She snatched the poster from the pole, hurried back to her car and drove through the intersection with her mind focused on seeing Gabe again.

When Liam McGregory entered the kitchen to fix the dish he was going to take to his second meeting with the Single Dads' Club, he came to an abrupt halt and scanned the mess. What happened? After putting away the groceries, he'd only left to wash up and check the mail. No more than ten minutes.

His seven-year-old niece, Madison, stood on a stool with a mixing bowl in front of her, dumping something that looked like sugar into it. Obviously she'd already put flour in, because the counter was covered in a dusting of white powder. Madison stirred whatever was in the dish while looking at a book next to her. "Milk is next."

On a chair pulled over from the table, Katie put a half-gallon milk carton down on the counter after pouring some into a glass and then passed it to her older sister. "Here." In the middle of the transfer, hands wobbled and the white liquid splashed all over the marbled-granite top, dribbling its way through the flour.

"I'm not gonna let you help me next time." Madison dumped what was left into the bowl, grabbed the carton and poured more straight into the concoction she was making. "You spilled most of it."

"You did, not me." Katie's expression morphed into her pouting one, her baby blue eyes narrowing. She snatched the milk from her older sister so hard more went flying out of the half-gallon container and splattered everywhere.

"Madison and Katherine McGregory, what are you two doing?"

Both girls suddenly twisted toward Liam, Madison's ponytail whipping around so fast it hit Katie in the cheek. Two sets of blue eyes, round as saucers, fixed on Liam.

Madison recovered quicker than her younger sister. "We're helping you, Uncle Liam. Aunt Betty said you've been working hard and we need to pitch in more." Her set jaw challenged him to disagree.

He inhaled a calming breath and moved toward his nieces, who he'd adopted when his younger brother died six months ago. "How you two can help me is to make sure the black Lab has water in his bowl out back."

The girls hopped down from their chairs at the counter and raced for the door to the backyard. Katie tried to go first through the entrance, but Madison quickly maneuvered herself into the lead. Only eighteen months separated them in age, but Madison was determined to make sure her younger sister remembered she was the oldest.

Before Liam began cleaning up, he needed to check that they weren't creating another mess outside, or they might never make the meeting for single fathers and their children started by the church his brother and nieces attended. He walked to the large window in the breakfast nook that afforded him a good view of his fenced-in yard. The black Lab came up to Madison and Katie, his tail wagging. His nieces lavished attention on the lost dog with no tags they'd found three days ago at the nearby park.

As far as his nieces were concerned, Buddy, their name for the dog, was theirs to keep. Reluctantly they'd agreed to help Liam put up posters about the lost Lab before he'd gone on his twenty-four-hour shift at the fire station yesterday morning. Liam had tried to explain to them that Buddy's owner was probably looking for him.

Buffalo had more than twenty thousand people but with a small-town feel to it. Residents looked out for each other. However, Madison and Katie were sure they were going to get to keep Buddy. Just another problem in the myriad issues he had been dealing with the past six months.

As Madison took the water bowl over to the outside faucet and filled it, Liam sighed and headed for the mess that needed to be cleaned up before he started dinner. How could two little girls manage to cover the whole counter on one side of a big kitchen with various ingredients in such a short time?

When his brother had died in that work-site accident, Liam's life had changed completely. Sure, he was still a firefighter. But everything else was different—new town, new family, new friends, new problems. When Gareth had asked him to be Madison and Katie's guardian if anything happened to him, he'd readily agreed, never thinking anything would.

Liam grabbed a wet washcloth and began wiping up the sugar-flour-milk mixture. When he peeked into the bowl, on closer inspection, he found a partially cracked egg in the middle of the concoction. He took the bowl to the sink and dumped it in the side with the garbage disposal.

Chimes rang in the air. The doorbell. Liam quickly checked on Madison and Katie then headed for the entry hall. When he opened the door, a petite woman with long blond hair framing an attractive face stood on the porch with a poster about the lost dog in her hand.

"Can I help you?" he asked, drawn to her dark brown eyes with their long, black lashes.

She smiled, and his attention zeroed in on her mouth and a dimple near its left side. "I hope so. I saw this on my way home from work, and I'm sure this is my dog. He's been missing for three days."

"Come in. I think I can help you. I'm Liam McGregory." He pushed the screen door open, and she stepped inside.

"I'm Sarah Blackburn."

She held out her hand, and Liam shook it. Her hair—a cascade of curls—instantly reminded him of his ex-wife. He stepped back, thankful she looked nothing like Terri.

He'd started to tell the woman about the dog they'd found, when the sound of the back door opening followed by running feet and a couple of deep barks announced his nieces as well as the black Lab heading this way.

Liam turned toward the hallway that led to the back of the house. The dog appeared and made a beeline straight for the woman next to him.

The black Lab lunged for her, propped his front paws on her shoulders and licked her. She had the biggest grin on her face.

"I thought I lost you." Sarah Blackburn hugged the Lab.

Madison halted by the entrance to the hallway. "Uncle Liam, we didn't mean to let him inside. He barged past Katie before we could catch him."

"I tried. Buddy is super fast." Katie, followed by Madison, moved to Liam.

He glanced at his nieces, who flanked him, staring at the woman hugging the dog. Tiny lines grooved their foreheads as they assessed what was going on. "I'm assuming from your welcome, he's your dog," he said, bracing himself for a protest from Madison and Katie.

The lady peered at him and nodded. "I didn't think I was going to find him. The few times he's gotten out of the backyard, he's always been on the porch when I came home from work."

Liam braved a glance toward his nieces. Katie's mouth hung open, while Madison's eyes glistened. "Girls, this is Ms. Blackburn, and the dog we found is…" He peered back at the woman.

"His name is Gabe. I live down the street on the next block," she said, gesturing in that direction. Then with her hand stroking the Lab, she calmed him and knelt next to him so she was more on the level with his nieces. "Have you two been taking care of him for me?"

Katie crossed her arms over her chest.

Liam prepared for her outburst, but instead Madison stepped forward and patted the Lab on the head. "Yes, we have. Are you sure he's your dog?"

"Here, let me show you." Sarah walked a few paces away and swung around to face Madison next to the dog. "Gabe, come."

The Lab walked to her.

"Sit," she said, and when he did, she ran him through some commands, which he performed.

"He knows tricks. We didn't know that." Madison crossed to them. "Can I try one?"

"Sure."

"Bud—Gabe, shake my hand." The dog held his paw up, and Madison shook it, grinning from ear to ear. "Cool."

"His name is *Buddy*." Katie stamped her foot, her lower lip sticking out.

Liam moved to her and placed his hand on her shoulder. "Honey, we don't want to confuse Gabe with another name."

"Buddy is friendly with everyone. We don't know for sure you're his owner."

"Katie, you knew this was a possibility. I talked to you about it." When he'd trained in Dallas to be a firefighter, he'd never received a course in dealing with a six-year-old losing something she had quickly bonded with, especially on top of losing her father six months ago.

"I tell you what. You all can walk with me to my house, and I'll show you a photo of Gabe and me. Will that prove to you I'm his owner?" Sarah asked in a calm, patient voice, as though she knew exactly what Katie was going through.

"I think that's a great suggestion, Ms. Blackburn." Liam caught the woman's gaze and, for a brief few seconds, a connection sprang up between them.

"Please, I'm Sarah. You have saved me hours of worrying about Gabe." She stuffed her hand into the large pocket of her light jacket and pulled out a leash. "I brought this to take him home with, but I see he managed to slip out of his collar again. It had all his information on it. Even when he wasn't on the porch, I thought for sure I would get him back right away."

"Then you can't walk him home. Without a leash, he might run off." Madison planted herself next to Liam.

"He'll be fine. He's well trained. He'll heel if I tell him," Sarah said, again in that even tone.

Her eyes narrowed, Katie lifted her chin. "What's that?"

"He walks on my left side right next to me."

Madison yanked on Liam's T-shirt. "Can we have a dog and teach him tricks like Gabe?"

He peered into Madison's pleading expression, meant to wrap him around her little finger. "I'll think about it, but first let's walk Sarah home. It's been a long day for all of us." Definitely an understatement for him with six different calls during the twenty-four-hour shift at the station that had ended at eight this morning. Two of their runs had been serious with one cutting a man out of a wrecked car. "Let's go, girls."

Madison hurried to be on one side of Gabe, sandwiching the dog between her and Sarah. Katie tried to walk right behind her older sister but kept running into Madison, who immediately swung around and pushed her back.

When Sarah stopped, her dog sat, and she looked at Katie. "Would you like to be over here with Gabe? You can be the one to tell him to heel if he tries to walk too fast or slow. I'll be right behind you with your dad."

"He's our uncle," Madison immediately said, frowning.

"Yeah and a firefighter. He helps people." Katie took Sarah's place by Gabe.

Madison glanced at him. "And he helps animals."

In that second all weariness from his last

shift evaporated. Sarah and his nieces had reminded him of why he worked crazy hours. But, mostly, it reconfirmed why he'd left everything he had known and come to Buffalo. The girls needed time to adjust to him before he moved them to Dallas. He'd told his captain he would return in a year with his nieces.

There were times he felt he'd made several strides forward with Katie but not necessarily with Madison when it came to their accepting him as their guardian. He was afraid losing the dog would set their relationship back. The death of his younger brother had hit them all hard.

"I'll be with your uncle and tell you when we reach my house."

Katie started forward, saying, "Heel," to Gabe.

Still scowling, Madison skipped a few paces to catch up with them.

"Did I say something wrong?" Sarah fell into step next to Liam.

"Madison is the oldest, and she's having a hard time accepting that her dad died. Katie's younger and seems to have accepted me as their guardian, most of the time. I don't do everything like their dad did." He'd tried, but he usually discovered he couldn't follow the same routine. His work schedule wasn't the same as Gareth's, who'd had an eight-to-five job with weekends off.

"Oh, I can imagine. My parents divorced, and when my father moved to Chicago, I rarely heard from him. What about their mother?"

"She died six years ago. Our aunt Betty helped Gareth with the girls and thankfully has been a lifesaver for me. She lives behind us, and when I'm working, she takes care of them."

"Betty Colton?"

He nodded. "Do you know her?"

"Yes, she comes every week to the hair salon I work at. I just moved back to Buffalo a few months ago when my mom needed help with my grandmother. We all work in the salon. Snip and Cut. It's been in the family for three generations now."

"Where were you before that?"

"Tulsa. How do you like Buffalo?"

"I haven't decided yet. I lived in Dallas all my life and love a big city." Liam stopped at the corner and waited while the girls checked both ways before crossing the street.

"My house is the white brick one with pink shutters almost at the end of this block," Sarah said as she and Liam trailed his nieces to the other side.

Madison twisted around and walked backward. "I love that house. Pink is my favorite color."

"Mine is purple," Katie said over her shoulder. "I hate pink."

"I don't have a favorite color. I can't make up my mind," Sarah said in spite of the glare Katie shot her way.

When Katie halted, Gabe did, too. "He stopped! Good boy." She petted his head then whirled around, her ponytail whishing. "I thought everyone had a favorite color. Why don't cha?"

Sarah shrugged. "I guess I'm the exception. I love all colors."

Liam wondered what else she was the exception to. Too bad he had little time to get to know Sarah. She seemed nice. But with his job and raising his two slightly rebellious nieces, he didn't. He'd always wanted to have children, and this would be the closest he would come to having a family.

"Uncle Liam, what's your favorite color?" Katie asked as she resumed walking.

"Blue."

Madison giggled. "No wonder. You're a boy."

A boy? He hadn't been one for years. At thirty-five he'd left his childhood behind in more ways than age. In his job he saw a lot of tragedy and was still trying to make sense of it. Look at all the deaths the two girls had dealt with in their short lives.

Sarah slanted him a look. "You okay?"

"Yeah. I was thinking about the last time I felt like a boy. Even as a kid, I was the man of the house. My dad was a firefighter, who died in an apartment fire when I was seven."

"And you wanted to follow in his footsteps?"

"Yeah. I knew I would be a firefighter when I first rode on the ladder truck as a kid. Even after Dad died, the guys from his station would come around and help Mom as much as possible." And he'd become a firefighter at that very station. When Terri had walked out on him, his buddies had been there to help him pick up the pieces.

"Girls, this is my house," Sarah called out and then turned to Liam to ask, "Would you all like to come in?"

Liam started to decline, thinking about the dish he needed to make before he and the girls left for the single dads' meeting at Colt Remington's ranch. But before Liam could answer, his nieces both said, "Yes."

As the others started toward Sarah's house, Liam hung back. He missed the guys from the fire station in Dallas. He hoped the Single Dads' Club would fill the void he'd experienced since coming to Buffalo. Even with Aunt Betty's assistance, he was alone, raising two girls who hadn't come with any instructions.

Chapter Two

When Sarah entered her childhood home, Gabe barked then loped toward the kitchen, where his food, water and bed were located. She showed Liam and his nieces into the kitchen while Gabe settled himself in his doggy bed. She checked the garage and wondered where Mom and Nana had gone. It was probably for the best her mom wasn't here. One look at Liam and she would try to figure out how to match them up. Her mother wanted grandchildren. Sarah wanted children. She'd been pregnant almost five months—until she miscarried after the car accident.

"Have a seat at the table. I have lemonade or iced tea. Which would you like?" she asked as she closed the door to the garage.

"Lemonade," Katie said while Madison replied, "Iced tea."

Sarah glanced at Liam, sitting across from the girls, a look in his golden-brown eyes—perhaps sadness—that made her wonder why he'd given up everything to move to Buffalo instead of taking his nieces to Dallas. It couldn't be easy becoming the guardian of two girls and also dealing with his brother's death and a new town and job. "How about you?"

"Thanks, but I'm fine. We can't stay long. I need to make something for dinner."

"Sure. I'll get their drinks then go find the photo." She turned to the refrigerator for the lemonade and iced tea.

Liam McGregory had the same color hair—dark brown—as the girls, but the similarities stopped there. Their eyes were a crystalline blue, his a warm brown. His facial features were angular and hard, while theirs were soft and delicate. She peered back at him, intrigued by what little she'd learned today.

A minute later as Sarah set their glasses in front of the girls, she caught Liam studying her. She hurried from the kitchen before he saw her blush. Since coming home to Buffalo, she'd avoided her mother's attempts to fix her up with a son of one of her friends. Sarah wasn't interested in dating, especially when memories of Peter bombarded her everywhere she went in town. She hadn't thought about that when she'd quit her job at a high-end salon, left her friends and returned home. Maybe that was why she felt a connection with Liam. He had to be going through some of the same problems she was, since he'd done the same thing when he'd come to Buffalo.

When Sarah found the photo with Gabe, she made her way back to the kitchen and put the frame on the table between Madison and Katie. The photo was of her Lab standing in eight inches of snow next to her. "Mom took that six weeks ago during the last winter storm. Gabe loves to play in snow."

"Me, too." Katie gulped down half her lemonade. "But I like swimming more."

"Yep, it's only…" Madison held her hand up and said, "April, May—" a finger popped up for each month "—two months to summer vacation. I can't wait."

"Not until I know you two can swim." Liam slid the picture frame across the table, looked at it and then gave it to Sarah.

She took it. "Did you know that the high school has an indoor swimming pool? In the evening, they have it open for swimming classes through their community outreach program."

Liam's gaze snared hers. "At this time of year?"

"Yes, especially now. A friend I grew up

with runs the program. I can give you her name. You can check to see if there are any openings left. Her next eight-week session starts in two weeks. I help her out two nights a week. I love to swim. It's better exercise than running."

Katie bounced up and down in her chair. "Can we? Can we?"

"I'll look into it when Sarah gives me the number, but you two know my crazy schedule."

"Ask Aunt Betty to take us." Madison drained her glass.

"We'll see. We don't even know if there are openings."

Although Madison didn't say anything else, her mouth tightened, and she stared down at her lap. For a couple of seconds it appeared as though Liam wanted to say more, but when he didn't, Sarah rose. "I'll write the number down for you." She moved to the desk under the wall phone and jotted the contact information on a piece of paper.

Madison clapped her hands. "Oh, goody. I know how to swim, but Katie doesn't."

"Yes, I do."

"No, you don't." Madison glared at her.

The noise of the garage door opening sounded as Sarah returned to the table and passed the paper to Liam. Now she would spend all evening answering questions about Liam McGregory. She contemplated trying to hurry the trio out the front door before Nana and Mom came in the back, but dismissed that strategy because if it wasn't Liam, her mother would home in on someone else. She just wasn't ready yet. She needed to get that point across to her mother.

"It won't hurt for both of you to take classes," Liam said as the door from the garage opened into the utility room. "Finish your drinks, girls. We need to leave."

Her mom's gaze latched on to Liam then drifted to Madison and Katie. A gleam lit her eyes. Sarah could almost see the hundred questions flying through her mom's brain right now.

Sarah faced the two women entering from the utility room. "This is my mom, Tina Knapp, and my grandma, Carla Knapp." She gestured to the trio. "This is Liam McGregory and his nieces, Madison and Katie. They live down the street and—" she swept her arm toward Gabe waking up and rising from his doggy bed "—they found Gabe. They put up posters. I saw one tacked to a telephone pole today."

Her mother grinned, put her purse on the

counter and shook Liam's hand. "That's great. Sarah has been so upset about Gabe being gone. We need to fix that hole in the fence better. Obviously what we did last time didn't work. I declare that dog of yours is like Houdini."

Katie scrunched up her face in a thoughtful expression. "Hou—denny?"

"One of the best escape artists, child," Nana said, her purse still hooked over her forearm. "My mother used to tell me about the time she saw Harry Houdini escape from a water container while handcuffed in a straitjacket and then lowered into it upside down. She said he was amazing."

"How did he do it?" Madison asked.

"By holding his breath three minutes while under water."

Madison's eyes widened. "Really?"

Nana nodded then took off her hat, something she insisted on wearing whenever she left the house. Sarah inspected her grandmother's legs that still showed a faint reminder of where the dyes splashed her. But the tennis shoes she wore were shiny white as if they'd just come out of their box.

"I took Mama to get a new pair for work. The others were ruined," Sarah's mother said as she sat at the table.

Liam smiled at her mother next to him.

Sarah had visions of her launching into her interrogation before he had a chance to escape. Sarah started to say something, but he stood.

"Girls, it's time to go. We still have to make something to take to the meeting." Liam turned to Sarah's mother and grandmother. "It was nice to meet you both. I'm glad Gabe is back home." Liam corralled his nieces toward the hallway so fast Sarah's mom could only blink.

Katie paused, signaled her uncle to bend down. She cupped her hand near his ear and whispered, loud enough that everyone heard, "I'm not glad. I'm gonna miss him."

"Shh, Katie. He isn't our dog." Liam was the last to disappear from view.

But Sarah heard Madison say, "We shouldn't have made those posters."

Sarah's mother laughed. "He has his hands full with those two. I've heard some stories from Betty about her grandnieces. So that's Gareth's older brother. Betty has brought them to church, but I haven't seen much of him."

Here come all the questions. "Liam is a firefighter and has a crazy schedule."

"Ah, yes." Her mom tapped the heel of her hand against her forehead. "I remember Betty telling me that."

"I'm going to my room," her grandmother muttered as she shuffled toward the hallway.

Sarah's mom waited a minute after Nana left, then said, "I had to take her back to the shop and make sure there was enough food for Sammy on the stoop. She was worried he would get hungry."

"That cat has to weigh twenty pounds."

"And Mama put most of those pounds on him." Her mother crossed to the fridge and poured herself some iced tea then retook her chair, peering at Sarah.

She sat across from her mom. Dark circles she insisted were from allergies highlighted the weariness in her mother's eyes. This was why she'd come home. She needed to remember that rather than get frustrated at her mother's attempts to play matchmaker. That first week back in Buffalo she wouldn't have stayed if she'd felt her mom hadn't really needed her. Not only had her health suffered, the salon had, too.

She sipped her tea. "It's a shame he can't join his nieces at church more. Gareth was there every Sunday."

"I think Liam feels a little overwhelmed with everything that has happened, being a single dad, new job and town."

"That's why he needs a woman." Her mom eyed Sarah. "Someone like you who is organized and a hard worker. Loves children."

Sarah held up her palm. "Stop right there, Mom. You'll get grandchildren when *I* find the right man, with no help from you."

"I'm not going to say another word about Liam McGregory today," her mother said. "I know it hasn't been easy coming back to Buffalo, but I appreciate your assistance."

Today was the only word Sarah really heard. What about tomorrow or the next day?

"Hon, I'm gonna need you to fill in for me on a committee I've been on the past five years. I don't think I would be very creative and helpful with all that has been happening with Mama these days." Her mother pushed to her feet. "In fact, let's order pizza. Right after dinner I'm going to head to bed."

"Nana had a bad day." Thankfully Sarah hadn't seen in the past eleven weeks she'd been home too many of that type of day. "Did she give you any problems at the shoe store?"

Her mother put her glass in the sink then turned, her mouth twisted into a frown. "Other than insisting on buying a pair of heels for work? No."

"I remember when I was a kid she always wore heels to the salon."

"But in the past few years she's worn tennis shoes. She'd break her neck if she worked in heels. Can you fill in for me on the committee?

It meets at noon at a restaurant downtown. For April and May once a week, or until everything is taken care of. The fund-raiser is June 4."

"I'll get the dates from you and make sure I don't have any clients scheduled at that time."

"We'll figure something out. The next meeting is this Tuesday."

"What's it for?"

"It's for the day camp at our church. It gives needy children in the area who can't afford the cost a chance to go. The fund-raiser kicks off the camp, which the kids can attend for June and July. Money is tight. For many working parents it's a lifesaver." Her mother headed for her room. "Will you order the pizza, please? I need to get off my feet."

Sarah watched her leave, not surprised her mother was on a committee planning for a fund-raiser for children. Sarah was an only child, not because her mother hadn't wanted more children, but because she couldn't have them. She knew the kind of longing her mom felt because she did, too. She loved children and would love to be a mother.

Running fifteen minutes late for his second meeting with the Single Dads' Club, jokingly referred to by some of the men as the Lone Wolves, Liam had to stop at a restaurant to purchase shredded barbecued beef on the way to Colt's ranch. They had stayed longer at Sarah's than he'd realized. There had been no time to cook. He remembered one of the firefighters at his station, Brandon Moore, had requested his homemade macaroni and cheese after Liam had served it for lunch last week. He'd intended to do that.

"We're late," Madison said from the backseat. "I hate to be late."

"So do I. See, we have that in common." Using the rearview mirror, he glanced at her and, as usual, she gave him a frown.

He sighed and kept his attention focused on the road leading out of Buffalo. When he'd first come to take care of them, Madison wouldn't even talk to him. At least now she did, although sometimes he wished she didn't, especially when she would point out that he wasn't her dad. He'd tried not to let those words hurt him, but they did.

"I like to be on time, too," Katie said right behind him.

"We have that in common, then." In the mirror he smiled at the six-year-old, who was missing one of her front teeth.

Why couldn't Madison be more like Katie? Earlier, when she hadn't wanted to give Gabe back to Sarah, had been one of the first times she had been difficult. The sisters argued all the time, but Katie hadn't argued with him. In fact, when he'd arrived to be their guardian, she'd latched onto him and had hardly left his side for the first month.

The main gate to the Remington Ranch came into view. Another car disappeared through it. Good, he wasn't the only one running late. As he turned into the ranch, a truck drove up behind him.

"It looks like others are late, too." He followed the Jeep in front of him, the road winding in an S with tall pecan trees on each side lining their path.

As they emerged from the green canopy, a large white house appeared, a veranda running the length of the front.

Madison whistled. "This is a big house."

"We're having a picnic out back, and then the kids can ride horses."

The sounds of cheers and claps filled the car.

"I guess you all want to ride?"

"Yes," they both said together.

Liam parked next to a white SUV and grabbed the food.

The girls hopped out before he had a chance to open his door and raced toward a group of kids. The last time they'd discovered several friends from school, so he'd hardly seen them the whole evening.

At a slower pace, he walked toward the food table.

Brandon came up behind him. "Macaroni and cheese?"

Liam set his dish with the others. "Nope. Didn't have time. The owner of the dog we found the other day showed up for him."

"How did the girls take it?"

"Considering they thought the Lab would be theirs forever, not bad. But I have a feeling they'll be bugging me every day about getting a new dog."

Brandon clapped him on the back. "Welcome to the club. My oldest son has had a string of pets over the years. If I let him, he'd open a zoo at our house."

Liam scanned the kids for Brandon's eleven-year-old son. "Where is Seth?"

He waved toward the rancher surrounded by six of the children. "He's bugging Colt to let the kids ride before dinner. I see your nieces found their friends."

Madison and Katie were in the middle of a group of girls. Colt's nine-year-old daughter stood next to Madison. The girl with Down syndrome grinned and nodded.

Colt stuck two fingers into his mouth and

whistled. The loud sound caught everyone's attention. "I told the kids we'll eat right now, so the ones who want to ride can *afterward.*" When a few children ran toward the food table, he added, "Let's say grace first." The three boys halted and bowed their heads as Colt blessed the dinner, ending with, "Give us the knowledge to do what is right, Lord. Amen."

When Colt finished the prayer, all the children hurried for the food, juggling for their places in line behind the fathers of the younger ones who went first to fix plates for their toddlers.

Fifteen minutes later the kids sat at a long table, the older ones a buddy for the young children. The dads settled in lawn chairs, close enough to make sure everything went all right while far enough away to talk freely about any problems they needed help with. Liam was between Colt and Brandon.

"Who wants the floor first?" Colt, the founder of the Single Dads' Club, asked the group. When no one said anything for a long minute, he smiled. "I'm not afraid to get this started. I freely admit I don't have all the answers, but I hope between us—" his gaze skimmed the faces of all eleven men present "—we can figure out what to do. Beth came home the other day crying. There was a birthday party last weekend, and everyone in her class was invited but her. It's hard seeing your little girl's heart broken."

"Confront the parents of the kid with the birthday," a man across from Colt said.

"No, you shouldn't do that. Have Beth ignore the child," another suggested.

For the next ten minutes different options were voiced. Liam listened to the men talk over a wide range of solutions, some he would never have thought of. "What did you do, Colt?"

"I held her then tried to take her mind off the birthday party. I'm not sure that worked. But y'all have given me something to think about. Anyone else have something they want to discuss?"

At the first meeting Brandon had told Liam about Colt's wife walking out on their marriage not a year after Beth was born. She couldn't handle their daughter having special needs. She'd disappeared with their son.

Liam was at least thankful he hadn't had children when his wife divorced him, but then, that was the reason why she ended their marriage. The last he'd heard, she was married and had a baby on the way. That was what she'd always wanted, but it hurt knowing he hadn't been enough for her.

"I feel out of my depth with two girls." Liam

finally said what he'd been feeling for the past six months. "They're different from boys. Do you find that a problem for you?"

Michael Taylor, a dad with two boys and one girl, chuckled. "Like day and night. What's going on at your house?"

"They insist on keeping their hair long. But you should see me trying to get it untangled in the morning before school. I suggested cutting it, but you would have thought the world was coming to an end. They were tardy for school that day."

"Do you have a detangle brush?" Nathan asked.

"I guess not. I don't know what that is. Where do you get it?"

"In the hair product section of the supermart. It was a lifesaver for me. Another dad with two daughters told me about it."

More problems and solutions were tossed back and forth until the children stood around looking at them because they couldn't go to the barn without their dads.

Colt rose. "I guess that's all for tonight. Feel free to call any one of us for help."

Suggestions for different situations filled Liam's mind. The first time he'd attended a meeting, he'd left numb with so much discussed and debated. This time hope bloomed inside him as though he might have a chance to make them into a real family.

All he needed was time and patience.

At noon on Saturday, Liam stuck the chicken casserole in the oven at the station house, set the timer for forty-five minutes and then refilled his cup with freshly brewed coffee. He headed for the patio behind the building to sit and enjoy his drink after a hectic morning.

When he'd returned from that multiple car wreck on the highway, he'd immediately started lunch while some of the guys had finished up cleaning the equipment and trucks. He'd become the cook on his shift after the others realized he knew how to prepare not just an edible meal but a delicious one, too.

Two other firefighters were outside on the patio. Brandon was stretched out in a lounge chair, catching some sun, while Lieutenant Richie Dickerson worked a crossword puzzle at the picnic table. He looked up as the door closing disrupted the quiet.

Liam took a seat across from Richie. "After we eat, I'll need to go to the store to stock up for next week. Earlier you said something about coming along, too."

The lieutenant put his pen on top of the *New*

York Times's puzzle. "Yep. I've gotta pick up some other items for the station."

"Are there any other errands to run?"

"Nope. That should be it today except for our refresher course in CPR at three. Of course, this schedule could be a moot point if an emergency comes up."

For the past two days both Madison and Katie had been moping around the house. Nothing Liam suggested for them to do was met with an enthusiastic response ever since Gabe's owner had retrieved him. And yet with him gone for twenty-four hours at a time, he was concerned about getting a pet for them.

"I do have a job for you. The captain suggested you could help Brandon with the fundraiser for the kids' summer camp. Every year we're one of the sponsors of the event, and we send two firefighters to be on the committee overseeing it."

Liam glanced at his friend, probably pretending to be asleep. "When are the meetings?" he asked, hating to have to ask Aunt Betty to babysit any more than she already did.

"That's the great part about it. It's during the weekday at lunch. If it's a day you're working here, you'll go as part of our community outreach."

"What if we are called out?"

"Usually, I can spare one, possibly both of you, depending on the emergency. On your days off, I still need you to attend the meeting. You'll get together once a week in April and May. The fund-raiser is scheduled for Saturday June 4."

"That's fine, since the girls will be in school. I think it'll be fun." Liam started to say more, when his cell phone rang. Hmm… Aunt Betty calling. Not good. She only called him at work when something was wrong. "Liam here." He steeled himself for what his nieces had done this time.

"I went out into the backyard to get the girls for lunch. They were playing in a fort they built out of blankets. But they're gone."

"You know how they love to play hide-and-seek."

"Liam, I promise I looked everywhere before calling you. They aren't at my house, and I even went over to yours, but they aren't playing in the yard there, either."

His brother had installed a gate between the two properties when, at three years old, Madison had tried to climb the fence to see Aunt Betty on her patio. "I'll be right there. You might talk to your neighbors and ask if they saw anything."

"I just went inside to make lunch. I brought

it out to have a picnic. I knew something was wrong when it got so quiet."

With his nieces, that was usually an indication they were up to something. When he hung up, he turned to the lieutenant. "Madison and Katie aren't where they're supposed to be."

"You go. I'll follow with a couple of the men." Richie strode toward the bay area of the station while Liam made his way to the parking spaces at the side and jumped into his red car, his heart racing.

What if someone had kidnapped them?

Eight minutes later he arrived at his house and noticed the girls' pink and purple bicycles weren't leaning against the back of the fence where they'd put them last night. The sight of them gone calmed him a little as he loped toward his aunt's yard. If someone had taken them, their bicycles wouldn't be missing.

At least he prayed that was true. He wanted the Lord to show him where they were, but he doubted he would hear from Him. He couldn't blame God. Liam hadn't had the strongest faith, and when his wife had walked out on his marriage, his life had fallen apart. Since coming to Buffalo, he was trying to change that because of his nieces.

Aunt Betty rushed out the back door. "A fire truck pulled up out front."

"A few of the guys are going to help us look for the girls."

"Should I call the police?"

"I don't think anyone took them. I think they went riding on their own." Liam rounded the side of his aunt's house toward the front with her following. He spotted his lieutenant and waved. "I'm going to drive my car around the area. The girls' pink and purple bikes are missing. They love the park two blocks away. Can you and the guys search there while I go up and down the streets?"

"Sure. If we find them, I'll call you on your cell phone." Richie turned to leave.

As the company of firefighters climbed back onto the engine truck, Liam headed toward his car.

Aunt Betty hurried after him. "I'm coming with you."

"No. Stay here in case they come back. You have my cell number. Call me. If I find them, I'll let you know."

"Oh, I hadn't thought of that. I'm so sorry. I should have made them come in when I did, but they were having so much fun with the fort."

The sorrow in his aunt's voice halted his steps. He hurried back to her at the gate between their yards. Tears filled her eyes. Her short graying hair wasn't its usual neat style but looked as though she'd run her fingers through it repeatedly. "This wasn't your fault. I suspect the girls wanted to go riding and left without asking you because you would have said no."

"Of course. They're too young to go by themselves, and I could never keep up with them while walking."

"I'm going to make sure they understand that when I find them." How, he wasn't sure. It was possible they rode to the park to play on the swings as they had yesterday evening with him. If so, Richie and the others would find them.

Driving about ten or fifteen miles per hour, he started down his street, going all the way to the dead end. He got out of his car and yelled their names into the wooded area near the creek. That was another place they loved to play, but there was no sign of them.

He started back the other way, inspecting every place he could. An invisible band around his chest tightened, threatening his breathing. When he reached the block Sarah lived on, he thought he spied the back end of a pink bike in her yard. He increased his speed, afraid to be optimistic. But as he neared, he saw the pink bike and then Katie's purple one.

He exited his car, praying they were at Sarah's. He rang the doorbell. No one answered. Stepping to the large picture window in her living room, he pressed his face close. Empty. He shouldn't be surprised. Most likely Saturday was one of her busiest days at the salon.

But if the girls are here, then where are they?

He reached for his cell to call Sarah at work. A deep bark echoed through the noonday air, and he stuffed his phone back into his pocket. He rushed around the side of the house and went into the backyard through the gate in the wooden fence. Giggles echoed in the quiet and spurred his pace. When he rounded the house by the kitchen, he found his two nieces lying on the grass, playing with Gabe.

Finally he allowed relief to loosen the tight hold tension had on him. He sank against the side of the house, watching his nieces so enthralled with Gabe they didn't even know he was there. He understood their attachment, but he couldn't let them think they could leave the house without a word to anyone. What should he do?

He took a step toward Madison and Katie, their laughter filling the air and wrapping around him. He hated to see it come to an end, but he had no choice if he was going to do his job as their guardian.

At the sound of the back door opening, Madison looked toward the deck and smiled. "Hi, Sarah. You said we could visit, and we figured Gabe was lonely while you're working."

Liam focused his attention toward the young woman, who had occupied his thoughts more than he wished these past few days since he'd met her. She glanced at him, puzzlement in her dark brown eyes.

He fortified himself with a deep breath. "Girls, you need to get your bikes. We're going home. Now." Amazingly he said it in a calm voice, but he'd learned in stressful situations that shouting didn't do any good.

Madison stared at him for a few seconds then whispered something into Katie's ear. Immediately both girls shot to their feet. Madison started for the gate at the side of the house while Katie bent and hugged Gabe before quickly catching up with her big sister.

When his nieces passed him, he said, "Wait by the car. I need to let Sarah know what happened."

"Uncle Liam, we didn't—"

"Madison, we'll talk when we get back to Aunt Betty's house."

Both girls slumped their shoulders and hung

their heads as they trudged the rest of the way to the gate.

As Sarah descended the stairs to the deck, commanding Gabe to stay, Liam called Richie and his aunt to let them know he'd found his nieces and would be back shortly. Sarah caught up with Liam as he exited the backyard to keep an eye on his nieces.

She looked him up and down in his fire-fighter uniform. "It's obvious you didn't bring them over here."

"No. I was at work when my aunt called to tell me they were missing. They left her back-yard and rode their bikes here without permission."

"I can imagine the commotion that caused. The neighbor across the street called when she saw you peeking into a window then heading for the backyard. She knows we work all day Saturday and…"

"Thought I was here to rob your place?" He grinned.

"Something like that. But when I saw the SUV and the bikes, I figured it was you. She'd called the police, and I managed to get hold of them before they arrived. They were on the way. My neighbor told me when I pulled up."

"Madison and Katie are good kids, but sometimes they act without thinking about the consequences. My aunt was beside herself with worry." Not to mention he was, too.

"Did you think someone abducted them?"

"Not when I saw their bikes gone. I'm sorry you had to leave the salon."

"No problem. I had a thirty-minute window to eat lunch. I'll grab something here and be back before my next client."

"Still, the girls need to apologize to you and Aunt Betty."

"I agree. I'll walk with you to your car."

He approached his nieces with Sarah next to him. Her presence eased the last remnants of tension in him. "Girls, leaving without letting anyone know was not okay. You scared Aunt Betty. You scared me. Sarah came home from work to check on who was at her house uninvited. What do you have to say to her?"

Katie mumbled, "Sorry," while staring at her tennis shoes.

Madison took in a deep breath and peered right at Sarah. "We just wanted to let Gabe know we miss him. I'm sorry."

"Okay, you two, into the backseat. I'll put your bikes in the trunk. I need to get back to work."

After he'd set the larger one in the trunk, Sarah picked up the smaller bike and handed it to him. "Have you thought of getting them a dog?"

"Yes, but I can't ask Aunt Betty to take care of a dog and the girls when I'm working. Dogs require more attention than other pets. After today, she might not want to watch the girls. I'm sure they added a few more gray hairs to her head."

"How about a cat? They're pretty independent. I seem to remember when I was a teenager that Betty had a cat. She used to talk about it with my mom when she came to get her hair done. She might not mind helping you with one."

"I'll think about it. But not for a while. They need to realize the seriousness of what they did." He walked toward the driver's-side door. Before climbing in, he twisted toward her. "Thanks for being so understanding about my nieces."

Liam opened the door and slid behind the steering wheel, then carefully backed out of the driveway since the trunk lid was up all the way.

Both girls cried out at the same time, "We're sorry, Uncle Liam," as if they had rehearsed what they had said. "We won't do it again."

"I'm locking up your bikes for the next week. No television, either. When you two disappeared like that, it scared Aunt Betty and me. We didn't know what had happened to you."

"But we're sorry and won't do it again. Promise," Madison said in a whiny voice.

Liam locked gazes with his eldest niece in the rearview mirror. "I'm glad, because next time I would have to take the bikes away for a month."

Katie's eyes grew round. "A month!"

"Daddy would never do that," Madison added.

After pulling into his driveway, Liam gripped the steering wheel until his hands ached. When Madison was really upset, she would invoke his brother. He didn't have a response to that. The mention of his brother just brought forth his sorrow once again at losing his only sibling and his inadequacies as a father figure.

Would he ever be able to follow in his brother's footsteps?

Chapter Three

After church on Sunday, Sarah changed into capri jeans and a T-shirt imprinted with a photo of Gabe then headed toward the garage to pick up the flat of pink impatiens she would plant under the shade of the oak tree. The day was too beautiful to spend inside. She relished her two days off. She worked hard, but she loved relaxing and gardening. She didn't cook much, but she could spend hours in the yard.

As she knelt on the ground under the tree, she turned the soil over, preparing to put the flowers in. Gabe sat beside her. But when the back door swung open, he stood, his tail wagging. She glanced behind her.

Madison and Katie, carrying pieces of construction paper, scurried down the stairs and made a beeline for her Lab. Then Sarah caught sight of Liam coming outside, her mom remaining in the doorway. Sarah's heartbeat kicked up a notch as it had done earlier when she'd glimpsed Liam coming into the church service late, his nieces flanking him. They'd sat in the back and left before she could welcome them. It had been the first time she'd seen him at the later service.

As the girls greeted Gabe, Liam cut the distance between them, grinning as he looked at his nieces, the papers in their hands plummeting to the grass.

Sarah rose. "What brings you by?"

He smiled at her. "After church, the girls had an idea to make cards telling you and Aunt Betty how sorry they were. We just came from my aunt's house."

"So that's what they have with them." Sarah winced when Gabe stepped on the card Katie had just dropped.

Katie snatched the card from the ground and tried to smooth it out, but there was a long tear in it. Her lower lip puckered as she stared at her work of art. Then she glanced at Sarah. "It's supposed to be for you." Her bottom lip stuck out even more as she handed it to Sarah. "I'm sorry."

"I love pictures of flowers. How did you know that?"

Katie shrugged. "I was gonna draw Gabe, but I didn't have time."

"I did." Madison placed her card on top of her sister's. "My teacher says I draw good."

Sarah quickly held one picture with the words "I am sorry" across the top of the construction paper in her left hand and the other in her right. "What a great idea! Thank you."

Katie thrust her shoulders back while Madison beamed.

Sarah peered at Liam. "Can you stay for some cookies? Mom made chocolate chip when she came home from church."

"Yes!" the two girls said in unison.

Liam chuckled. "I'd have a riot on my hands if I turned your invitation down."

Madison moved forward, her attention shifting between Liam and Sarah before she asked, "Can we play with Gabe?"

"That's for your uncle to decide."

"For a little while." As Katie ran across the yard to pick up a tennis ball, Madison hurried after her while Liam added, "I didn't mean for our visit to interrupt what you're doing."

"The ground is ready. All I have to do is plant the impatiens. That won't take long. Besides, they're doing me a favor. Gabe could spend all afternoon running after that ball. After fifteen minutes my arm gets tired. This way everyone is happy." She removed her garden gloves and started for the house. "I'll bring some lemonade, too."

When she entered the kitchen, her mother was in the middle of the room, her hands on her waist, facing her grandmother. "Today isn't a work day, Mama."

Sarah glanced at her grandmother, dressed in the hat she usually wore to the salon as well as one of her plain dresses that had become her uniform when at work.

"Yes, it is, Tina. If we don't hurry, I'm going to be late. I have a shampoo to do. I don't like to keep Marge waiting."

"We went to church this morning. It's Sunday." Sarah's mother's voice rose.

Nana shook her head. "We didn't. I would remember that." She pointed at the calendar on the side of the refrigerator. "I checked that. Today is Saturday, April 2." She tapped the date. "See it hasn't been crossed out yet."

"Nana, I forgot to mark off yesterday. Sorry." Sarah took a black marker and slashed an X through the date. "A friend and his two nieces are here to visit. The same ones who rescued Gabe this week. Why don't you come out and have some lemonade and chocolate-chip cookies with us?"

For a few seconds confusion clouded Nana's

eyes before she switched her attention to Sarah's mom uncovering the cookies. Chocolate chip was her favorite kind. "I guess so. If you're sure this isn't Saturday."

Sarah nodded. "I'm going outside on the deck. Madison and Katie are playing with Gabe."

"I need my floppy hat and to change into long sleeves. I can't be in the sun too much." Nana glanced once more at the calendar then left the kitchen.

"I'll bring it out, hon. Go entertain your guests." Her mother reached into the refrigerator, pulled out the pitcher of lemonade and set it on the counter.

Sarah started to protest, knowing exactly what her mom was doing—trying to put them together. Then she realized the uselessness in attempting to explain. She'd just met Liam, and he was dealing with a lot right now. He might not be the biological father of the girls, but he was a good father—the type she would like for her own children. She gasped. That thought came unbidden into her mind and took her by surprise. She certainly wasn't hunting for a husband right now.

"Is something wrong, Sarah?" Her mother retrieved some plastic glasses from the cabinet.

Sarah crossed to the back door. "No." Especially if she made sure to keep those kinds of thoughts to herself. That would be all she needed if her mother thought she was interested in Liam. If she'd learned one thing coming back to Buffalo, it was that her running away from her hometown after Peter had died had only delayed her dealing with his death.

Outside she joined Liam, who sat on the deck steps. "By the time I came out of the church service this morning, you and the girls were gone."

"We would have gone to the early service with Aunt Betty, but Madison kept changing her clothes. She had to look a certain way. A lot of her friends attend there. Do you always go to the eleven o'clock one?"

"Yes. I can't get going much earlier than that." As Sarah lifted her arms to rest them on her thighs, she touched Liam's. Her breath caught. She should have sat on the bottom stair instead of next to him, but she hated having to twist around to talk to him and then back to watch the girls and Gabe.

"I have to admit when I arrived at Aunt Betty's at eight this morning, all I wanted to do was go home and sleep. We had to fight a fire in the middle of the night. I thought of having them just go with Aunt Betty, but after the stunt they pulled yesterday, she needed some time without them. We went home so I could change from my uniform, and Madison decided to change her outfit *five* times. I'm not sure if she was stalling or what, but I was determined we would get to church even if we went to the later one and I was exhausted. Gareth always took them and, when I'm not on duty, I try to do what he did."

"Did you get any sleep?"

"An hour. I'll be going to bed at the same time they do tonight. I'm still working on getting this daddy gig down."

She thought he was doing a good job, considering six months ago he had been a bachelor with no children. Taking on a ready-made family overnight wouldn't be easy for anyone. When a husband and wife had a baby, they had nine months to prepare. Liam hadn't had any time. "I could watch the girls for a few hours while you catch up on some sleep. I could have them help me plant some flowers, and then we could go to the park with Gabe."

"I can't ask you to do that."

"You didn't. I volunteered."

"But—"

"I'd love to. Gabe enjoys them, and that way he won't be pestering me to throw that ball all afternoon." She gestured toward Madison and

Katie taking turns tossing the tennis ball for her dog.

"If I hadn't been exhausted before this, I would be now watching him running after it over and over. How old is he?"

"Seven years old. In his heart he still thinks he's a puppy. When he crashes, he'll sleep for hours then want to do it all over again. Much like a child, he wants attention, but Mom and I work often from eight to six, five days a week. When we come home after being on our feet all day, we're tired, and he's ready to play all night."

"That sounds like me when I have a shift where I work most of the time, like yesterday's. All I want to do is crash onto my bed and catch up on sleep. Usually the kids are at school, but not when I work Fridays or Saturdays, which is every two weeks."

"What happens when the kids are out of school in a couple of months?"

Liam rubbed the back of his neck. "I haven't figured that out yet. Aunt Betty has been wonderful, but she is seventy-five. My girls can run rings around her."

She loved the way he referred to Madison and Katie as his girls. He might be their uncle, but he was settling into the role of being a father well. She wondered if he had ever been married. Instead she asked, "Was your brother younger or older?"

"Younger by three years. I'm thirty-five, and I know better than to ask a woman her age."

She laughed. "If I can ask, then you can, too, but I'll save you the bother. I'm twenty-eight." When the sound of the back door opening announced her mother was joining them, she glanced over her shoulder, wishing she had chosen to sit farther away from him than she had. It didn't take much to encourage her mom to matchmake.

"If you're sure about letting the girls stay, I'll grab a cookie—" a twinkle sparkled his eyes "—or two before I leave and tell my nieces where I'm going."

"They may not want to stay."

"Are you kidding? I heard them plotting in the kitchen after church. Katie was sure I'd bring them over if they made cards for you."

Sarah rose. "It seems your youngest niece knows you well."

"You mean she has me wrapped around her little finger. I admit sometimes she does, but I wanted to see you again so I agreed after only a little begging." He leaned close to her ear and whispered, "But don't tell them."

"They won't get it from me." She turned to

the yard and called, "Do you two want some cookies and lemonade?"

Madison had her arm in midthrow and stopped. The ball plopped to the ground near her, and the girls raced toward the deck. Liam stepped to the left while Sarah moved to the right. Madison and Katie ran between them and skidded to a halt at the glass table. Just as she and Liam were going to close the gap between them, Gabe loped by.

"I have some wipes you can use to clean your hands." Her mother handed each one a cloth.

Sarah looked up at Liam. He chuckled then said, "They came to me that way. They go full throttle like Gabe then crash hard—" he checked his watch "—in about five hours."

"If I only had half that energy." Sarah walked toward the table, watching the smile on her mother's face as she poured the lemonade and made sure the girls had enough cookies. Gabe lay down between Liam's nieces, probably hoping to lap up the crumbs that fell on the deck.

When Sarah and Liam sat, her mom scrutinized him as she took a chair next to Madison. Sarah braced herself for the interrogation that would probably follow.

"Liam, I understand you haven't been living here long. How do you like Buffalo?" her mother asked while his nieces were busy finishing their first treat and starting on another.

"It certainly is different from Dallas." He took a bite of the cookie. "Mmm. This is delicious. Better than the ones I make."

Her mother's eyebrows shot up. "You bake cookies?"

"I didn't set out to be a cook, but in Dallas that became my job at the fire station. I'll admit I liked doing that more than cleaning the place. Over the years I've kept adding recipes to what I can prepare. I figure if I'm going to cook, I should do it well. The guys on my shift here quickly put me in charge of the meals."

"We used to eat out a lot. Not now. His pizza is the bestest I've had." Katie's legs swung back and forth as she stuffed the last of the second cookie into her mouth.

"I love his fried chicken." Madison patted her stomach. "Oh, and macaroni and cheese. It's not from a box," she added in astonishment.

"I like to cook, too, but alas, my daughter doesn't. I'd love to share recipes. The chocolate-chip recipe was my mother's."

"Mom, Nana should be out here by now." Sarah hoped she took the hint and went inside to see about Nana before she started asking Liam more personal questions.

Her mother frowned and pushed to her feet. "You're right. She's having one of her days."

After her mom went inside, Liam asked quietly, "Is your grandmother okay?"

"Some days she forgets things."

Although she had kept her voice low, Madison heard what Sarah said to Liam. "I forgot how to spell Buffalo on my spelling test, but I remembered Oklahoma."

"That's great, Madison." Sarah was glad the girls didn't start asking questions about Nana's memory, and she would remember in the future even when they didn't look as though they were listening, the girls were probably paying attention.

Katie sat straighter. "I know how to spell my whole name."

Madison jumped to her feet. "Ready, Gabe."

The black Lab stood, his tail wagging.

Katie snatched another cookie and started to follow Gabe and Madison.

"Girls, I'm going home in a few minutes." Liam finished his drink and put his glass on the table.

Madison whirled around. "You can't. We wanna play with Gabe more. He wants us to."

Katie nodded over and over.

Liam rose. "I know. Sarah thought you could stay here for a while then go with her to the park with Gabe."

"After the park, I'll take you back to your house. Today is just too pretty to spend inside," Sarah said as the back door opened and her grandmother and mother appeared.

"In fact, when you three come to my house, I'll have dinner almost ready, and if Sarah wants to eat with us, that's fine with me." Liam peered expectedly at Sarah.

"How can I turn down that invitation? I'd love to."

Madison put her hand on top of the Lab's head. "So Gabe can stay at our house, too?"

"Yes, while Sarah is there." Liam smiled at Nana, who had on her floppy hat but was still in her work clothes with short sleeves.

The girls charged down the steps to the yard and ran toward the tennis ball on the ground near the back fence.

"Who's this young man?" Nana asked as she took a seat. "I haven't met you before. Are you sweet on my granddaughter?"

Heat flooded Sarah's face. There was no telling what her grandmother would say. On her good days she wouldn't have said that so bluntly. She usually was the subtle one.

"We're friends, Nana. Liam found Gabe when he was lost."

"Gabe was lost?" Her grandmother chewed on her lower lip, trying to think.

"Yes, a few days last week. Mom, will you keep an eye on the girls while I show Liam out?"

"Sure. Take your time."

The urge to roll her eyes at her mother was strong, but she refrained from doing it. Instead she walked with Liam around the side of the house and through the gate. When they were in the front yard, she said what she hadn't wanted to say with his nieces nearby. "Nana is eighty and has bouts of forgetfulness. Today is one of those times. When Mom asked me to move home to help her at the salon and with my grandmother, I couldn't turn her down. Family is important to me."

"I agree. Now if I can just figure out this daddy thing, life will run much smoother."

"I don't know if that will ever happen, but you're doing fine."

He smiled. "You're kind. You didn't see me trying to get my nieces to move this morning when we were late for church."

"It happens to all of us."

"I'm beginning to see that when I hear the

stories some of the guys talk about at my single dads' group."

"Networking is important. I'm looking for a group for caregivers that my mother can join. I think she would appreciate the support and a place to talk about her problems. We talk, but it's not the same thing. I haven't yet gone through the problems she has, but I can stay home with Nana while she attends."

"There isn't one at church?"

"No, but maybe Mom could start one. That's a great idea, Liam." She heard the gate open and watched as the two girls raced out of the backyard with Gabe right behind them, barking.

Madison skidded to a stop first, excitement on her face. "You've got to come look." She tugged on Sarah's arm while Katie tugged on Liam's. "You won't believe it."

Chapter Four

As Katie pulled Liam toward Sarah's backyard, he didn't know if he should prepare himself for something bad or good. With his nieces, he had trouble reading them at times, but at least it was better than the first month he was here. The girls would go from crying one moment to laughing the next. Their emotions had been all over the place, but then, so had his. He didn't have a large family, and Gareth's unexpected death had overturned his world.

"Just wait and see, Uncle Liam. You won't believe it." Katie kept tugging on his arm, determined to beat her sister to whatever they wanted him to see.

But Madison was several steps ahead of them. Sarah glanced over her shoulder at him, giving him a puzzled look, her eyebrows lifting.

He shrugged and shook his head.

Madison dragged Sarah around the back of the shed. "Look at them. They are so cute!"

Katie dropped his arm and raced ahead.

Liam came into view of the two girls and Sarah sitting on the ground while five kittens explored them.

"Where's their mama?" Madison carefully picked up one, black with white markings, and rubbed her face against its fur.

Sarah scanned the area. "I don't know. There was a pregnant cat that used to visit my yard every day in the evening when Gabe was inside, but I don't know if it was a stray or belonged to someone. She was mostly white."

"Like this one." Katie gathered a white kitten, except for its black tail, in her lap and stroked it.

"Yes. She must be the mama. Maybe I can ask around the neighborhood to see who owns the cat." Sarah examined a white, brown and black kitten.

Liam took a place across from Sarah, his nieces flanking her. "Why would she leave them? They don't look more than seven or eight weeks old." A brown and black kitten climbed onto his legs.

"She wouldn't unless they somehow got away from her or…" Her forehead furrowed.

"Or what, Sarah?" Madison asked.

"Something happened to her. These babies look well fed and cared for. They haven't been on their own for long."

Katie lifted the last kitten, white with brown markings, and put it in her lap. She looked right at Liam. "Could we take care of them until she comes back?"

Liam had no idea how to take care of cats, let alone kittens. Growing up all he'd had were dogs. "If we took them home, the mama wouldn't know where they were."

"Oh, you're right." Katie frowned, petting both kittens in her lap. Then suddenly her eyes brightened. "We can make posters to find their owner and mama." She glanced at Madison. "We're good at that."

"That's a great idea. Your poster led me to Gabe." Sarah looked around. "Where is he?"

"Your mama took him inside when she saw the kittens. She told us to get you. She was sneezing. Is she sick?" Madison cradled her kitten against her chest.

The white, brown and black one began climbing all over Sarah. "She's allergic to cats but mostly the pollen in the air. She can't be around outside long in the spring."

"That's sad." Katie said while both of her

kittens began playing in her lap. She giggled. "Then we have to take them."

Those words struck panic in Liam. He hadn't figured out how to raise two girls, let alone five kittens.

Sarah caught his gaze and smiled. "They should stay here. I can make a place in the shed for them. You two can help me this afternoon."

A scowl descended on Madison's face as she set her squirming kitten on the ground. "What about Gabe?"

"Gabe is usually great with other animals. We'll figure it out. What I'll need from you two are some posters. What do you say?"

"Uncle Liam, will you help us like you did last time?" Katie asked.

He could do this. "We'll start after dinner tonight, and then after school tomorrow we can finish them and put them up."

"I can help, too. Monday is my day off. Until then we can clean the shed and make it safe for them—" Sarah's eyes gleamed "—while your uncle goes home. I'm looking forward to his dinner tonight."

The girls hopped to their feet as Liam stood and offered Sarah his hand. "Are you sure you don't need my help?"

She stepped closer while the girls corralled the kittens. "Yes. I know an exhausted man when I see him. Everyone needs a break once in a while. Besides, I don't have men cooking dinner for me too often. Go. We're gonna be busy this afternoon, and you'll only get in the way."

"Yeah, Uncle Liam. This is women's work."

Liam shot a look at Madison. Where in the world had she heard that? "Okay, I'll leave you *women* alone. Dinner will be ready by six."

As he strolled toward the gate, Liam heard Katie say to Madison, "We aren't women. We're kids."

"We *are* women," Madison said in a raised voice.

He slowed his pace, sure he would have to go back to break up another argument.

"Actually you are both women. Or, rather, females and children. Madison, will you ask my mom for a box from the garage? Katie, I need you to keep an eye on the kittens while Madison gets the box. I'm going to check out the shed."

Madison hurried toward the back door while Katie kept her attention fastened on the kittens. As Sarah rounded the front of the shed, her gaze connected with his. For a brief moment Liam felt rooted to the spot by the gate. He liked her, and he could tell the girls did, too. She blinked and severed their link. Waving her hands, she shooed him away.

When Liam opened the front door to let in Sarah and his nieces, the aroma of beef, onion and something she couldn't place flooded her senses. Her stomach rumbled and the girls giggled.

"You must be hungry." Madison charged into the house first.

While Katie rocked back on her tennis shoes, she stared up at her uncle. "Gabe is staying at Sarah's. He's babysitting the kittens."

"He is? They get along?"

Katie nodded as if she were an authority on the Lab. "Yes. In fact, when he lay down, he let them climb all over him." Katie moved into the entry hall. "And I'm hungry, too. When are we eating?"

Liam looked at Sarah and grinned. "I guess we're eating first."

"Is it ready?"

"It will be after they set the table and wash their hands. I stuck the rolls in the oven right before I answered the door."

She took another deep whiff of the dinner. "What is it?"

"I came home and put a meat loaf in the oven, cut up the vegetables and put them on to simmer slowly while I grabbed a much-needed nap. How were the girls?"

"Great. They worked extra hard on the shed. Katie told me she wanted the bestest place for them."

"They didn't complain."

"Not once."

"How did you accomplish that? I get at least groans and moans if I ask them to do something around the house. The worst is when Madison points out to me that their daddy never made them clean their rooms or pick up their mess in the den." Liam stepped to the side to let Sarah inside.

"Really? Do you think they were telling the truth?"

He shut the door, turned toward her, looked over her shoulder and then leaned close and whispered, "They're listening. Yes, I do, because when I arrived in Buffalo the house was a mess. Gareth hated cleaning up as a kid."

"But you did?" His nearness sent her heart thumping against her rib cage.

"Yes. What I didn't learn as a child, I did when I went to work at the fire station. My captain was a stickler for it. A place for everything. That cut our response time down by a minute over other stations."

"But you might not be able to run this household like a fire station."

"It makes good sense in any situation."

She remembered what Nana had told Mom when Sarah was young. "There is a time for work and a time to play. Don't sacrifice one for the other. At least, that's what my grandmother used to say. I don't know for sure. I don't have kids."

Liam turned to the living room where the girls were hiding. "Madison, Katie, that's enough listening to our conversation. Why don't you two go set the table?"

Madison stepped into full view. "I don't wanna." She crossed her arms and tilted her chin up. "Katie hardly did anything last time."

"I did, too." Katie pushed her older sister.

"Now." Liam raised his voice.

"Daddy never—"

"Enough," he said, cutting off Madison.

"I will, Uncle Liam." Katie spun around and hurried toward the kitchen.

"Thank you, Katie," he called out then stared at Madison.

"You like her better than me." His niece stomped after Katie.

Liam released a long breath, kneading his nape. "Their idea of helping is making a bigger mess."

"Have you let them know what you expect?" Sarah wished she could erase the lines of concern on his face.

"I just did."

"Not exactly."

When he frowned, confusion carved deeper lines in his features.

She took his hand, tugged him into the den across from the living room and faced the entry hall to keep an eye out for any little girls trying to listen. "You gave them a choice when you said 'why don't you two set the table.' Any time you phrase something you want done in a question, they have a choice. Yes, they will or no, they won't."

"So I should have said 'go set the table.'"

"Yes, exactly."

"How do I convince Madison I love her the same as Katie? I gave up my life in Dallas to come here and raise them."

"Talk to her. Find out why she doesn't think you do."

"It's probably because I get on her about chores more than Katie. Her sister doesn't give me as much grief as Madison does."

"Remember this is all new to both of them. They won't change overnight. Madison is the oldest. She's been doing it one way longer than Katie."

He plowed his fingers through his hair. "I wasn't prepared for this."

"Even though they still live here in the same house, it is a big adjustment for them. Everything in their surroundings is familiar except you."

Memories of living in the same place after Peter had died brought the sorrow of that time to the foreground. She started to share it with Liam so he'd know she'd gone through something similar, but the words wouldn't form in her mind. Instead she added, "They expect to do everything the way they always have here. Show them your way one step at a time. Give them time to get used to a few chores before you give them any more."

"Are you sure? You don't have children. I can't keep messing up."

For a moment she didn't breathe as she dealt with the deluge of emotions of when she'd lost her unborn baby. She couldn't say anything. She turned away, tears blurring her vision.

"I'm sorry. I didn't mean that as a criticism." He clasped her shoulder. "Please forgive me. Lately I've been making one mistake after another."

She swallowed hard, squeezed her eyes closed a second and slowly rotated toward him, his hand slipping away. The words she'd wanted to tell him about having a miscarriage and how hard that was stayed locked away. She rarely talked about it, even to her mother. "I was married for three years, and we were hoping to have a family but my husband died in a car crash."

His expression morphed into a look of regret. "My frustration caused you to remember, and I'm so sorry for that and for your husband's passing."

Stamping down the pain, she continued, "I do have some experience dealing with children. As a teenager, I worked in a day care center to earn money in the summer, and I volunteered at the church nursery during the late service. Also, I'm the designated hairdresser for the children who come to the salon."

He smiled. "Good. When I can convince the girls to have their hair cut at least a few inches, you'll be the one I come to."

Behind Liam, Madison and Katie appeared in the doorway. Sarah indicated them with a nod.

Liam turned. "Are you two ready to eat?"

"Yes, and we're starving. I've even washed my hands already." Katie held them up still wet.

Madison didn't say a word. She stalked toward the kitchen.

Katie took Liam's hand. "She doesn't want her hair cut. She wants to see how far it will grow." The child looked at Sarah. "But you can cut mine."

"That would be great. Your uncle can call to set up an appointment with whatever works for you two."

The little girl grinned and took Sarah's hand, too. Her daughter wouldn't have been much younger than Katie if she'd lived. Again Sarah fought the emotions threatening to take over. She wasn't going to ruin their evening because she hadn't worked through her grief. Instead she'd run away from it, but she was discovering that that didn't really work.

A half hour later, everyone sated, Liam put his napkin on the table. "I have dessert. We can eat it in the den while working on the posters, if you all want."

Katie's eyes grew round. "We can?"

"I thought we couldn't eat in there." Madison pinched her lips together.

"So long as you clean up any mess you make, I don't see why not." He recalled his first month with them and the food he'd found everywhere, some with mold growing on it. That was when he'd put his foot down and restricted eating and drinking outside the kitchen. He was going to try this. Maybe Sarah was right.

Madison's solemn expression eased. "In our bedrooms, too?"

Apparently his brother had let them. The memory of the half-eaten grilled-cheese sandwich under Madison's bed with ants crawling on it taunted him. He had second thoughts. He wasn't sure if he should allow them to take food upstairs. "How about we try downstairs for a month, and if you clean up after yourselves, then I'll let you also in your bedroom? But again, you have to take care of any mess you make. Okay?"

"Yes!" Katie pumped her arm in the air.

"What if we don't, or Katie doesn't and I do?"

"Then Katie can't take food or drink out of the kitchen. You can." Liam slid his gaze to first Madison then Katie before it settled on Sarah. The smile she sent him warmed him. He felt as though he'd taken a step in the right direction.

Madison took the last bite of her meat loaf. "Sarah, I want to help with the kittens. I hate seeing them in the shed all day."

Katie dropped her fork on the plate, the clinking sound echoing in the kitchen. "You can't let them out. They could get lost. If their mama comes back, they won't be there."

Madison glared at her younger sister. "If you would let me finish, I have a solution. After school we could come down and play with them in the backyard."

"And Gabe," Katie inserted quickly, receiving another glare for interrupting again.

"I know you'll be tired after working all day, so you need us to care and feed them. Also to play with Gabe," Madison said in a rush then blew out a large breath.

Sarah's gaze riveted on Liam. "What do you think?"

"We could, at least the days I'm home, but I hate to ask Aunt Betty."

"We can, can't we, Madison?" Katie asked.

His eldest niece nodded while her teeth dug into her bottom lip, a sign she was nervous, unsure.

Liam wanted to erase Madison's worry. She struggled to figure out what she was feeling. "It'll only be for a while until they're placed in homes if their owner doesn't come forward first."

"Maybe a month or less. I'm okay with it if your uncle is. I know Gabe would love to see you." Sarah turned her attention to Liam.

This was a chance for him to bond with his

nieces. He couldn't pass it up. "I'm all-in. But I don't want you both to become too attached to the kittens. I haven't talked to Aunt Betty about getting a pet yet."

"We won't." Katie glanced at Madison. "Right?"

"Nope. Gabe might get jealous if we only play with the kittens."

"Good. Any of the days from Tuesday through Saturday that you all can come will be a bonus for Gabe and the kittens." Sarah asked, gathering up the plates, "What's for dessert?"

"Banana pudding. Nothing fancy." As she continued stacking the dishes, he captured her hand as it reached for his utensils. "What are you doing?"

"Cleaning up the table." She scanned their faces then winced. "Sorry. A habit. At our house whoever cooks doesn't clean up. The others do. So it falls to me and Nana. My mom always insists on cooking, and I gladly let her."

"Hmm. An interesting policy. What do—" He started to ask the girls if they wanted to do that but stopped. He realized he was asking a question that would no doubt elicit a big no from both of them. "Tell you what. Girls, one of you clears the table while the other puts them in the dishwasher. I'll rinse them off. And one day a week, you two will be the cook.

With some help from me. You've been wanting to learn." The memory of the concoction they'd recently made shivered through his thoughts.

"And you'll totally clean up that day?" Madison asked, doubt in her voice.

He nodded. "I think it's time I teach you both how to cook."

Katie clapped while Madison scrutinized him for a long moment before saying, "Yes."

"But for tonight, we'll all clear the dishes, and I'll clean them up later. We don't have a lot of time before you'll need to get ready for bed. It's a school day tomorrow."

Both girls hopped to their feet, took some of the dishes Sarah had stacked in front of her and set them on the counter by the sink.

"Can we get the supplies out?" Madison asked.

"Sure. I'll dish up the dessert and bring it into the den." Liam checked the wall clock. "We only have an hour."

His nieces ran from the kitchen.

He waited a minute, glancing toward the doorway. "I've had to fight them every meal so far. What do you think? Will this work?"

"Hopefully, but knowing kids, there will be some slipups. Be prepared for them."

"Yeah, with Madison, I'd be surprised if she didn't. She loves to test me."

"Most kids do."

"That's what the guys in my single dads' group told me the first time I went." He rose. "Do you want dessert?"

"Yes, I love banana pudding. Do you use vanilla wafers in it?"

"That's the only kind. I used to eat half of it in one sitting. That frustrated Mom until she started doubling the recipe." He opened the refrigerator and removed a bowl. "I'll bring yours and the girls' into the den."

"Then I'll go see how they're doing."

When she left, Liam scooped some pudding into four bowls and set them on a tray with spoons. As he made his way to the den, he thought back to what Sarah had told him before dinner about losing her husband. That had saddened him. Hopefully she would get the chance to be a wife and mother again in the future. He'd eventually learned to accept that he wouldn't father a child, but it had taken time. From her expression when talking about it, he didn't think she had accepted the loss of her husband yet. He'd accepted that Terri left him three years ago, but he still couldn't forgive her for how she'd done it.

As he neared the room, Madison said, "I can't believe he's gonna teach us to cook."

"Why do you want to learn?" Sarah asked, stopping Liam a foot from the door.

"Because Daddy did. She wants to do anything he did. What do you think of this kitten?" Katie's voice grew more excited as she spoke.

"A pink cat? That's ridiculous."

Before a fight ensued between Madison and Katie, Liam stepped into the den. "I hope you're hungry. There's nothing left for seconds." He set the bowls in front of them and took the chair across from Sarah.

Katie held up her poster. "There's nothing wrong with this."

"Pink will catch a person's eye." Sarah held her hand out for the paper. "I'll print the information on it while you make another one."

Madison snorted. "Well, I'm gonna do the correct color."

Liam inspected the two she'd done so far. "Those are nice. Let's try to do about ten tonight. We'll make a few more tomorrow and then hang them up to see if anyone comes forward."

For the next hour Liam worked with Madison while Sarah helped Katie, who insisted on putting glitter all over the poster. His eldest niece grumbled a couple of times under her breath; otherwise the conversation was dominated by Katie telling Liam everything she'd done to help Sarah today.

He glanced at his watch near eight. "It's time to call it quits for the day. We did even more than I thought we would. We're a good team."

"Some of us are." Katie glared at Madison.

"I'd like one for the salon. I'll put it where everyone will see it when they come in. The problem is picking one. They're all great."

Madison shot to her feet. "I'm going to bed." She snatched up her bowl and stomped out of the room.

Katie giggled. "That means you can take mine."

Sarah's gaze latched on to Liam's. "Since there are extras, is it possible if I take two of them? One of Katie's and one of Madison's? I can't decide between them, and I have two places they can go."

He wanted to applaud her answer. He'd been trying to come up with a way that would leave both girls happy. This parenting thing made him feel as though he was trying to find his way through a smoke-filled building—progressing slowly, not sure of where he was going. "Go ahead. We can always make more if we need to."

"I'm glad you're using the pink cat." Katie stood, took her bowl and left.

"I'm sorry about Madison. Lately instead of adjusting better, she's getting worse. She gets angry at the smallest thing. Aunt Betty told me both girls used to be so close. She doesn't understand this change, especially with Madison toward Katie."

"Suppressed grief will sometimes have that effect on a person. Has she seen a counselor after her father died?"

"A couple of times, then she refused to go. Counseling isn't effective if the person doesn't want it. I'll let her know that option is still available."

"That's all you can do. I'd better go." She started to grab her bowl.

"I'll take care of it. I really appreciate your help this evening." Liam pushed to his feet at the same time Sarah did. "I'll see you out."

When he stepped onto the porch, he peered around. "Where's your car?"

"At home. We walked here from my house."

Liam stared at the darkness that surrounded them, except for the dim illumination on the porch and the streetlights. "I don't like you walking home alone without Gabe."

She chuckled. "It isn't that far, and Buffalo is different from big cities. I'm safe. When I can't swim for exercise, I've walked before at night after work, and I've never been afraid."

"If you're sure. I can get the girls down here—"

She put her hand on his shoulder for a second. "I'm sure. Thanks for offering, and for these." She waved the posters.

Although she'd removed her hand almost instantly, his heartbeat revved into double time. Since coming to Buffalo, he hadn't gone out on a date, even when Brandon had tried to fix him up on a blind date. He'd had too much to deal with, and he hoped to return to Dallas with his nieces in six months.

"Good night. The dinner was great." She descended the stairs to the sidewalk.

He watched her until she disappeared from his view. If he dated here in Buffalo, it wouldn't be Sarah. Although he was attracted to her, she wanted children someday. He saw it every time she was with the girls.

That was one thing he couldn't give a woman.

Chapter Five

On Tuesday, Liam slid into Brandon's F-150 truck, their fire equipment in the back in case there was a fire they would have to respond to. Since showing up at the station that morning, Liam had wanted to pull Brandon to the side to talk to him about what was happening with Madison. He had two sons close in age and might have gone through the same problem.

Brandon pulled out of the parking space. "You've been awfully quiet this morning. Something going on?"

"Girl problems. Madison is fighting with Katie more and more. I thought things would settle down after a few months getting used to me as their guardian. Katie is doing pretty well. Madison's reverted to the way she was that first month I came to Buffalo, and I don't know why."

"Have you asked her?"

No, he hadn't. Why not? "I did try when I first came, and she would just clam up. According to her, everything was fine. Actually *peachy* was her exact word."

"Peachy? I wonder who she got that word from."

"Aunt Betty, no doubt."

At the stoplight Brandon looked at him. "I'm not sure what works for a boy would be the same for a girl. My oldest was so angry when his mother died. I tried to talk to him, and he wouldn't have anything to do with me. Then Nathan in the single dads' group told me he needed to learn to release that anger. Both his kids were going through it. With his son, he got him involved in karate as an outlet for his feelings. You'll need to ask Nathan what he did for his daughter because, as you know, they don't think like us. Give him a call."

Liam chuckled. "That's for sure. I'll call him before World War III erupts in my house."

"Usually my sons get along, but for a while after Mary Ann died, they were at each other's throats. Each wanted my undivided attention without the other around."

That could be the case. He seemed to do more with Katie because she asked. What if

Madison was jealous or upset that she wasn't getting equal time? "So what did you do?"

"Each week I plan something special for each one. I make arrangements for the other to stay with a friend or family member."

"I can't ask Aunt Betty to babysit any more than she already does."

"Go the friend route, then, or I know a good babysitter on my block that you could use." Brandon drove into the parking lot at the side of the Redbud Cafeteria. "Let me know, and I'll give you her number. She's sixteen and very reliable."

"Thanks. This gives me something to try." Liam climbed from the truck and headed for the restaurant entrance. "How long are these meetings?"

"It'll depend. Since this is the first one, it could go on for a long time if we can't decide what our fund-raiser is gonna be. This is my third year. The first year we had a three-hour lunch full of arguments. But once we have a plan, things start to move fast."

After Liam followed Brandon through the cafeteria line and selected his lunch, they made their way to a back room where the meeting would be held. Half the seats had been taken. Liam scanned the faces and saw the Buffalo

Community Church's pastor sitting there next to Sarah.

She's on the committee? She didn't say anything to me about it. Since finding Gabe, he'd seen Sarah more often than most people. At least with her here, he knew three people on the fund-raiser committee, although it might make it harder to back off from Sarah.

There were empty chairs at the second table. Maybe it would be better to sit apart from her. "I see some places—"

"Let's go," Brandon interrupted when he spied Pastor Collins.

His friend headed for the empty seats across from the pastor, and Liam had no choice but to accompany Brandon, especially when Sarah caught sight of Liam and smiled. The warmth in her expression, followed by Liam's heartbeat quickening, shouted to him to run away before he let her into his life too much.

"I didn't know you would be on the committee," Sarah said as he sat directly across from her.

"I just found out a few days ago."

"So did I. Mom usually represents the church with Pastor Collins, but she has her hands full with Nana these days."

Pastor Collins inclined his head. "It's nice

to see you again, Liam. Brandon and I are old hands at this."

After pleasantries were exchanged, Liam dug into his chicken-fried steak with mashed potatoes while Brandon carried on a conversation with the pastor. He satisfied himself with several bites before he looked up to see the seats were filling up. Then he made the mistake of glancing at Sarah.

Her dark brown eyes gleamed at him. There was no way to avoid Sarah. Even if she'd been sitting across the room, he'd be drawn to her. "How is your grandmother doing?"

Sarah took a sip of her iced tea then set it down. "Actually the past couple of days she has been doing well, but we never know when she'll go through a 'spell,' as my mom refers to her forgetfulness. How about your nieces? Since you're working today, I gather they won't come by this afternoon."

"No, unless they can talk Aunt Betty into it. I told them if they didn't say anything to Aunt Betty, I'd make sure we visited Wednesday, Thursday and then Saturday."

"Great. I know Gabe and the kittens will like it. I was out in the backyard yesterday, and they had a ball."

"Anyone contact you about them?"

"No, except one lady told me she'd love to

have a kitten. Recently one of her cats died. She's coming this weekend to pick one out."

Liam cut another piece of his meat. "That's good. One down and four to go."

"Are you going to take one?"

"I hate to ask Aunt Betty to take on one more thing. She doesn't complain, but she's so tired when the girls leave her." He sipped his iced tea. "So I'm assuming no one has come forward about the mama."

Sarah ate the last of her chicken potpie. "No, that's why I think the stray cat that used to come by is their mama. Nana particularly liked her visiting. She had a cat before moving in with Mom. I think it would be good for Nana."

"Has your mother thought about getting allergy shots, or maybe you can keep one of the kittens as an outside cat?"

"Then, in cold weather, it could stay in the garage."

"It might work. See, you'll have the kittens taken care of in no time," Liam said as an older gentleman stood, walked to the head of the room and raised his hands to indicate everyone be quiet.

The fiftyish man turned out to be the mayor. From the crowd in the meeting room, Liam gathered this fund-raiser was important to the townspeople.

"For the new people on the committee, the first thing we need to decide is what kind of fund-raiser we're going to have," Mayor Adams started off. "In recent years we've had a rodeo, an arts-and-crafts fair and a carnival. We don't want to repeat those, so we need some new suggestions."

"A talent contest," a lady in the back shouted.

"Or a garage sale," an older woman suggested. "I have tons of stuff I'd like to get rid of."

Brandon leaned toward Liam and muttered, "But would anyone want to buy it?"

"A silent auction" came out of Liam's mouth before he realized he'd actually spoken.

All eyes were on him, and he wanted to squirm in his seat. He hadn't intended to say anything, since he was new to the town and the fund-raising committee, but he remembered attending a silent auction in Dallas. It had been well received and had raised quite a bit of money for the charity.

Sarah grinned then said to the group, "I like that. We could have a dinner and sell tickets to it. During the evening, items can be displayed for people to bid on, then at the end have a bachelor auction to wrap up the fundraiser. I've heard in other places they can be quite successful. I attended one in Tulsa, and it brought in a lot of money."

"We've had some where I'm from, and they were popular." Liam didn't add that single firefighters were often asked to participate in the bachelor auctions.

"I like that idea the best. Something a little different," Brandon chimed in, with several others agreeing.

The mayor twisted his mouth into a thoughtful expression. "Okay, but in the past we've tried to let all ages participate in some way in the fund-raiser. If we have a sit-down dinner, is it for adults only? I saw one on television once, and it was fancy. Black tie and everything."

Sarah rose and faced the committee. "It can be either fancy or casual. We can have different classes at the school or a softball team or any group of children donate baskets for the auction. It's a great way for kids to give to other kids. The dinner can be a buffet or waiter service. We could use teenagers to be the servers."

"Let's vote. We have several choices," Beatrice Miller said, sitting next to the mayor.

"Okay. A show of hands for a talent show." Mayor Adams counted the few who voted. The garage sale got a couple of more raised hands for the fund-raiser, but the overwhelming majority wanted a silent auction/bachelor auction combo.

Pastor Collins stood. "We can use the church's large hall off our kitchen for the dinner. At one end we have a stage where the bachelor auction can take place. The corridors and entrance would be a great place to set up the items for the silent auction. I would suggest myself, Sarah Blackburn, Liam McGregory and anyone else who is familiar with this type of event be on the planning committee. We can meet and come back next time with what subcommittees we'll need, then you all can sign up to be on one or two of them."

When Liam heard his name included, he wanted to shout no. *I don't know what I'm doing with my nieces, let alone a big fundraiser!* He couldn't shake the sensation of being steamrollered, and he felt overwhelmed just thinking about it.

As several people raised their hands to be added to the planning committee, Liam leaned toward Brandon. "Is Pastor Collins always like this? He didn't even ask me if I wanted to do this."

"Yep, usually in a more subtle way, but this sounds big and with the potential of bringing in more money than we have in the past. We should have started last month. When he sees a job that needs to be done, he digs right in." Brandon grinned. "You'll be fine. So many of us have a job on the side when we aren't at the fire station. You don't, so you should have plenty of time for this. Look on the bright side, the kids are still in school so it will be easier."

Liam chanced a look at Sarah. Her eyes were as round and large as the wheels on the ladder truck. For a few seconds that bond he'd felt before sprang up between them. They were in this together—reluctantly.

When Pastor Collins took his seat, Liam bent forward. "I'm new to town. I don't know that many people. I may be more a hindrance than a help. You should get—"

"Nonsense. You and Sarah will be a fresh perspective for us. We need new people, otherwise some will take over and do the same old thing. We'll make sure we meet on a night you're free." The pastor swung his attention to Brandon. "How about you? We could use another man on the committee." He lowered his voice. "You know how Beatrice Miller can be."

Liam glanced at the woman next to the mayor. She'd captured the ear of the man and was waving her hands around. Liam elbowed his friend in the side. "Yeah, how about you? We're on the same shift."

"Sure, I can do it if I don't have problems getting a babysitter for Seth and Jared."

"I don't mind having the meeting at my house, and you can bring Seth and Jared over."

Sarah's invitation surprised Liam. He swung back toward her. "How about Madison and Katie?"

"Fine. I have a feeling the kittens and Gabe will keep the children entertained. If not, my mom and Nana will be there."

"Then let's meet Thursday night at six thirty. Is that all right with y'all?" Pastor Collins rose.

Sarah, Brandon and Liam all nodded.

"I'll go tell the other members. I'll need everyone there so we can plow through the details to bring before the whole group next Tuesday." The pastor hurried off to talk to the others.

Brandon pushed to his feet and clapped Liam on the shoulder. "Ready to leave?"

"Yes, but I need to talk to Sarah for a moment."

"I'll be outside."

When Brandon left, Sarah scanned the area then asked, "Is something wrong?"

"Are you sure about having the meeting at your house?"

"Positive. I'm hoping Seth and Jared will

take one look at the kittens and want one. Besides, my mother loves kids and will get a kick out of watching them. We have a great floodlight, and they can be outside for an hour or so, then they can use our big den, where they can watch TV and play games if the meeting runs late. Nana will love it, too."

"Okay. I was going to volunteer my house, but with your mom there it'll be much better. And this way I can leave before it gets too late. With it being a school night, the girls will need to be in bed at least by nine." Liam started walking toward the exit. "I still can't believe Pastor Collins volunteered me. I wasn't even sure when Richie asked me to be on the committee."

"Notice we're the only ones younger than thirty-five in the planning group. And Beatrice will definitely try to run the whole thing."

"Good point."

"Have you ever participated in a bachelor auction before?" Sarah stepped outside.

"Yes, once in my younger days. It was for a great cause."

"How did it go?"

The memory of his ex-wife, Terri, standing up in the room full of women and putting in the last bid for him chilled him in the warm April afternoon. "I brought in two hundred dollars for the charity." He glanced at Brandon sitting in his truck. "I'd better go. See you Thursday night." Liam would never have suggested a silent auction if he'd known where it was going to lead the committee. Now he would see Sarah *more* often not less.

He wasn't sure how he felt about that.

Sarah sat behind her steering wheel, watching Liam and Brandon leave the parking lot at the restaurant. When she asked about his participation in the bachelor auction, she sensed she'd hit upon a touchy subject. The date must not have gone well. At least he'd only had to go out once with the woman and, as he'd said, it had been for a good cause.

She checked the clock on the dashboard and hurriedly started her engine. Her next appointment at the salon sometimes came early and hated being kept waiting.

Ten minutes later she pulled up at the back of the shop. Nana sat on the stoop, watching Sammy eating the food she'd put out for him. Her grandmother loved this part of the day. Maybe Sarah would talk to her mom about checking into the allergy shots and coming up with a way to keep at least one kitten. Having a pet was good for a person. She'd realized that when Peter died. Gabe had gotten her through some bad times.

"Hi, Nana. Is Sammy letting you pet him yet?"

Her grandmother tilted her head and studied the white tomcat. "Not yet. But I'm patient. Today I've got a treat on the step next to me."

"Good strategy. Get him used to you. It might work."

"You know the white kitten looks like Sammy except for that one smattering of black on his tail. I think I'll call him Junior."

Sarah leaned down and kissed Nana's cheek. "I love you. If you need anything, I'll be in the kitchen until my client comes."

"That's good. I came out here because Betty is here and complaining about her aches and pains. She's younger than I am, but the way she's been carrying on, you would think she was older." Nana shook her head and held up the treat for Sammy to see where she placed it. "She might take one of your kittens. She saw the poster and asked about them."

Great. If she could get Brandon to take one for his boys, Liam to take one for his nieces, one for the lady coming this weekend as well as Nana, that would mean all of them would have a home. Then she wouldn't have to worry. As she entered, the sound of her mother and

Liam's aunt Betty talking drew her toward the main part of the salon.

"Why, Tina, you're downright devious. What if your daughter finds out what you did?"

Sarah stopped and ducked back into the kitchen before the two women saw her. What had her mother done?

"I made Captain Pierce promise he wouldn't tell Liam I called and requested he be on the fund-raiser committee. I've got to do something, or Sarah will be an old maid."

Old maid? Not possible. *I've already been married.*

"I want grandchildren, and she isn't getting any younger."

Embarrassment seared into Sarah's cheeks. She was only twenty-eight not forty-eight.

She was about to interrupt their conversation when Betty said, "I don't know how much longer I can care for the girls. It takes the two days Liam is around to recuperate from having them for twenty-four hours. Don't get me wrong—they're sweet kids. But for Gareth I would watch them a couple of hours until he came home from work. That was so much easier."

Poor Liam. No wonder he was extra careful not to cause his aunt any more work than what she was doing.

"If we could get Sarah and Liam together, that would solve both our problems," her mother said over the sound of the blow-dryer.

Sarah's marital status was *not* her mom's problem. She balled her hands, her fingernails stabbing her palms.

"Yes, hopefully by summer, when Madison and Katie are out of school."

Her mother chuckled. "Then we have our work cut out for us."

"I'm going to see if I can get the girls to help. Those poor children need a mother."

The bell over the front door rang, indicating someone was coming into the shop.

While her mother greeted Sarah's next client, she took several deep breaths to restrain herself from charging into the room and confronting her mom and Betty. A minute later she entered the shop as her client took the chair in Sarah's booth. She decided not to let her mother know she had overheard her talking with Betty.

Not until she talked with Liam.

Late Wednesday afternoon Sarah pulled into her garage with Nana. Her last client had canceled, so she'd left the salon early. She needed to talk with Liam about what she'd overheard yesterday. She hoped he and the girls were still here. Her grandmother was functioning well and could keep an eye on Madison and Katie playing with the kittens.

All last night she'd kept tossing and turning, rehashing the conversation between Mom and Betty.

She wasn't ready to date. Although she had dated a little in Tulsa, returning to Buffalo had made her feel as though the accident had happened recently. She didn't know if she should have a talk with her mother or just ignore all her plotting. Maybe Liam could figure out what to do.

The sound of the car door opening pulled Sarah away from her dilemma. Nana swung her legs around to stand.

"Wait, Nana. I'll help you."

"Nonsense, Sarah. I'm perfectly capable of getting out of the car on my own. If I could just get Tina to understand I can, just at a slower pace." Nana gripped the seat and door frame and pulled herself upright. "See. I'm not totally falling apart."

"She doesn't think that."

"Hogwash. I haven't forgotten how to walk. I can walk circles around her."

Sarah pressed her lips together to keep from chuckling at the image popping into her mind. When she unlocked the door to the house, she let Nana go in first then followed her. She immediately hurried to the back window in the alcove and spied Liam and the girls. She sighed.

"Nana, can you watch Madison and Katie while I have a word with Liam privately?" She looked over her shoulder at her grandmother with her hat on and her purse hooked over her lower arm.

A twinkle lit her blue eyes. "I will, and I won't even tell Tina you wanted to talk to Liam alone. It'll just fuel her meddling."

"Why do you say that?"

"My hearing is just fine, too. I heard her and Betty Colton talking about getting you and Liam together. Tina doesn't realize how loud she is at times."

Sarah closed the space between them and hugged her. "You're the best. Thanks!"

Her grandmother set her purse on the kitchen counter, removed her hat and started for the door to the deck. "I'll sit under the oak while they play. Those two are adorable, but something is bothering that older one. What's her name?"

"Madison. And I think so, too."

When Sarah stepped onto the deck with Nana, Liam swiveled around. Surprise widened his eyes as his gaze tracked slowly down her, as though making sure she was all right. His perusal left her slightly breathless.

"The youngest is Katie," Sarah whispered in a raspy voice to her grandmother as they descended the stairs to the yard.

Liam checked his watch as he walked toward them. "You're home early. I thought for a second we'd overstayed our visit, which, with those two, wouldn't be that hard. They are masters at delay tactics."

Nana smiled. "It's nice to see you again, young man. I'm sitting over there." She gestured toward the folding chairs under the big oak tree.

"I need to talk to you—" Sarah took his hand and pulled him toward the deck "—out of earshot of a couple of little girls."

"This sounds serious. Have we been kicked off the committee?"

"In your dreams. No, this is about my mother and your aunt."

"Oh." He stretched his long legs out in front of him as he settled into a chair on the deck.

Too charged to sit, more from his look earlier, Sarah remained standing. "Nana is watching the kids while we talk, but to be on the safe side we should probably stay nearby."

"How's she doing?"

"Today was great. On Monday, Mom took her to the doctor. He sees Nana every three months. He changed her medication. Yesterday was a good day, too. Maybe this new medicine will help her."

"So what's going on with your mother and my aunt?"

Sarah glanced over her shoulder to make sure the girls were at the rear of the yard, playing with the kittens. Gabe stood nearby, keeping an eye on the babies, which he'd decided was his role in their lives. "When I went back to the shop yesterday, Betty was getting her weekly wash and set. I came in the back way, and they didn't know I was there or I'm sure they wouldn't have been talking about us."

His eyebrows slashed downward. "Us?"

"We're on the committee because Mom orchestrated it. Once she had me taking her place, she called your captain and asked him to assign you to be one of the firefighters working on the fund-raiser."

Liam's expression went blank for a few seconds, then storm clouds brewed in his eyes. "How does Aunt Betty fit in?"

"My mother was recruiting her to help get us together. She gladly joined forces to see us as a couple."

The firm set of his jaw emphasized the tic in his cheek. "I should have hired someone to keep the girls rather than continue having Aunt Betty watching them. I didn't—still don't—

want to disrupt their routine any more than I have to. What do we do?"

Sarah finally sat next to him. "I don't know. It's all I've been thinking about."

"We can't quit the committee, and I really don't want to. Once I make a commitment, I stick with it."

"Me, too. I just hate being manipulated by Mom."

"Okay. We're on the committee and now know what's going on. Just because they wish it, doesn't make it true."

"Right," Sarah said, and yet for a few seconds she wondered what it would be like dating Liam. He certainly was good-looking. But the quality she liked in him the best was his caring nature. "Should I have a talk with Mom about this?"

"Beats me. I'm still trying to figure out my nieces. Madison's birthday is in a couple of weeks, and I'm not sure what to do. I've never planned a birthday party for a little girl."

"I'll help you. I haven't, either, but I was a little girl once. It'll be fun. When is it?"

"April 23. It's a Saturday and I'm scheduled to work. I'll check to see if I can trade a shift with someone on the Friday before."

"If you can't, we can have the party on Sunday afternoon."

"I don't want to miss Madison's birthday."

"You won't if we do it that way."

He sat forward, resting his elbows on his knees. "I mean the actual day, especially the first one with her dad gone. Birthdays in my family were always important. I'm sure they were that way with Gareth. I've gotten photos of some of his productions."

"Oh. Like what?"

"A bouncy house. A magician to do tricks for the guests."

"This is how you celebrate your birthday?"

"Not anymore. I was never as big about it as my younger brother. How about you?"

"We went out to dinner and I had a cake. Occasionally, I had girlfriends over to spend the night. Mom doesn't even want her birthday acknowledged."

He laughed. "We were raised on two different planets."

Sarah scanned the backyard. Nana was with the girls, holding the almost-all-white kitten. She was definitely going to talk to her mother about keeping that one. Once it was big enough, it could be outside most of the time. "What would you like to do for Madison?"

"Something a little different, but I'm not sure what."

"Let me think about it." She already had

some ideas but didn't want to say anything until she did some checking to see if she could pull it off. She would have to rebook her standing Saturday appointments, too.

"You know we still haven't come up with what to do about your mother and my aunt."

"Again, let me think about it. I don't want her to think she can manipulate me in the future, but she's always been one determined woman."

"And now that we know what she's up to, we can throw up roadblocks until she gets the message."

"That might work, but my mom really wants grandchildren. She wanted a house full of kids, but couldn't have any more after I was born. I could say I was brainwashed from an early age, but not really because I love children and want to be a mother."

For a few seconds she thought about telling him how her miscarriage had affected her, but that she hadn't given up hope she would have a family one day—just as soon as she worked her way through her grief.

"I do, too, that's why—"

"Katie, get down from there. You're gonna fall," Madison shouted from behind the shed, a frantic ring in her voice.

Chapter Six

Liam leaped to his feet and, with a quick visual sweep of the yard, took in Madison standing near a large crab apple tree, holding two kittens and staring up. Nana, holding two other kittens, approached his eldest niece. As he charged down the steps, he couldn't see Katie or the fifth one in the litter.

"Where is Katie?" he shouted when he was halfway to Madison.

Turning to him, she pointed to the crab apple. Tears streaked down her face. "One of the kitties got away from us, and she went after it. I didn't know it was up in the tree."

As Sarah joined Liam, he scanned the flowering branches and spotted Katie near the top. His heartbeat thumped rapidly against his chest for a few seconds before he went into firefighter mode, as if an emergency was part of his life every day.

"Katie, stay where you are." He headed toward the base of the tree, glancing at Madison. "She'll be okay and so will the kitten."

Sarah slipped her arm around Madison, who leaned against her, still crying.

"But I can't get to Blackie. She's scared," Katie said over the cries from the stuck kitty. "Uncle Liam, she's the one I like the bestest."

"I know." The crab apple was nearly thirty feet tall and twenty-to twenty-five-feet wide. Liam assessed the weight the branches between him and Katie could take. "You come down, and I'll get Blackie."

"I can't. She'll get scared. She's shaking."

All he saw for a moment was the fear in Katie's eyes, her teeth digging into her lower lip. "Stay still, then. I'm going to get a ladder."

"Please hurry. I don't want her to fall. I was paying attention to another kitten and didn't see her leave."

He had a ladder at home, but maybe Sarah had one. "I'll be right back." Liam motioned to Sarah.

She slipped her arm from Madison and hurried to him. "There's a ladder in the garage that I use to clean the gutters. It might work," she said before he could ask.

"Can you keep an eye on her? I'll get it and be right back." He already started for the back door, knowing that both of his nieces were in good hands with Sarah.

He quickly found the twelve-foot ladder, hoisted it against his side, punched the garage door open and hastened around to the backyard. Gabe sat between Nana and Madison, who moved closer to the tree, all of them talking to Katie.

As he reached the tree, Sarah sat on the bottom limb, a few feet closer to Katie. "I got stuck in a tree once. A kid dared me to go all the way to the top. I got halfway and a branch I held snapped off. I clung to the tree until help came."

Liam settled the ladder against the other side of the crab apple where it fit better as Katie asked, "Did you ever climb trees again?"

"Yes, but only when I was sure it was big enough for me. That's why I'm staying on this bottom branch. The upper ones might not hold my weight like it will for you."

The fear he'd seen in Katie's eyes had faded as she held on to the main trunk of the crab apple. The kitten's cries still filled the air, spurring him faster before either one did something dangerous. From his side he climbed a few feet higher as his youngest niece's gaze latched on to him.

When he reached the last rung of the ladder, he smiled at Katie. "It's been a while since I've been up in a tree. It's like looking out your bedroom window on the second floor."

Katie turned her head from side to side. "I don't like it. Too high."

"I'm going to help you scootch around to the ladder. Once you're on the ground, I'll get Blackie."

"She's scared like I am." Inch by inch Katie came around to the other side of the tree then set one foot on the branch near the ladder.

While Sarah and Madison held the ladder steady at the bottom, Liam poised halfway on the ladder and the biggest limb nearby. "Give me your hand."

Katie clutched a close branch while she reached for Liam's fingers. When he clasped her, she edged forward.

"You're almost there. A few more inches," he said, guiding her toward the ladder.

Katie grasped the top rung, swung around and placed one foot on it. Liam adjusted his hold so if she slipped he could grip her better and prevent her from falling. Katie glanced down, and her eyes widened.

"Katie, look at me. Sarah is holding the

ladder still. Put your other foot on it then your hands."

Slowly his niece did as he said and clung to the ladder.

"I knew you could do it. Now go down to Sarah, and I'll get Blackie."

When Katie was close to the ground, she hopped off the ladder and shouted, "I did it. Get Blackie, Uncle Liam. Please." Then she fell into Sarah's arms and hugged her.

Liam's gaze linked with Sarah's and for a brief moment the world fell away and they were the only two people around. He wanted to get to know her better. Not only did animals respond to her, his nieces did, too. She had so much to offer.

"Uncle Liam," Katie called out, pulling away from Sarah and peering up at him, "don't forget Blackie."

He blinked several times and swiveled toward the kitten on a thin branch about a yard away from him. He held out his hand and said in a coaxing voice, "Come on, Blackie. You can get down."

The kitty looked around then issued a loud cry.

"Okay, then I'll come up there." Liam inspected the branches surrounding Blackie and decided one was thick enough to hold his 180 pounds. He hoped.

He reached for a limb above to help steady him as he climbed. Then he looked around for another so his weight would be distributed. When he found one bigger than a pinkie finger, he started his ascent. As he searched for a foothold, he put more downward pressure on the branch he held in his right hand.

Snap.

He teetered on the limb while grasping for another one to hold.

The sound of gasps drifted up from below.

"I'm okay." He stabilized himself and took a deep, composing breath.

"I'm sorry. I'm sorry."

Katie sobbed the words, ripping his heart in two. "Honey, you have nothing to be sorry about." He glanced down at her to reassure her. Both girls' arms were wrapped around Sarah while Gabe and her grandmother kept an eye on the other four kittens.

He hated to think how the girls would take it if something happened to Blackie. *Lord, I need Your help. Please.*

He reassessed the path he needed to take. At least Blackie was terrified enough that she wasn't moving. Again he began talking to the kitten in a soft, soothing voice as he shifted direction and scaled the tree from the other side. Finally he made it to within an arm's length of Blackie.

"See, I told you I would get you. Stay still while I reach for you."

Blackie quieted her cries and listened as Liam continued to reassure her while at the same time leaning toward her and plucking the kitten from the branch. Sagging with relief, he cradled the soft ball of fur to his chest.

An idea popped into his head. He unbuttoned his shirt partway and placed Blackie between it and his chest. He felt the sharp dig of the kitten's claws and stroked his hand down her back.

"You're okay. Stay there and we'll both be on the ground in a minute." He prayed his calm words would convey the right message.

As he scrambled to the ladder, Blackie settled down and retracted her claws. When his feet touched the ground, his nieces swarmed him. He withdrew the kitten from under his shirt and knelt in front of Katie, putting the kitty into her hands.

She took Blackie then plastered herself against him. "You are the bestest, Uncle Liam. Thank you."

"Sweetheart, next time come get me."

"I will. I promise." Katie gave him a kiss

on his cheek and then took Blackie to see the others.

Sarah stepped to his side. "I'm glad that lady is coming this Sunday to take one of them. Less to keep an eye on. That happened fast."

"With kids it often does—at least, that's what I'm discovering." His right hand hurt, and he looked at it. "I didn't even realize I'd scraped my hand on a branch."

Sarah took hold of him. "Let me get something to clean that."

"You don't have to. We need to leave soon, anyway."

"It's no problem. It's the least I can do. You're helping me with these kittens." She started for the house. "Be back in a sec."

Inside Sarah closed the kitchen door, leaned back against it and dropped her head. She stared at her shaking hands. When Liam had slipped and had to catch his balance, her heart had plummeted. Seeing him almost get injured only reinforced in her mind that she wasn't ready to put herself out there emotionally again to marry. She didn't want to lose another man she loved.

As she made her way to the bathroom to fetch the peroxide and a Band-Aid for his palm, she couldn't stop visualizing him falling out of the tree and hitting the hard ground.

She gripped the counter and stared at her reflection: white as a sheet, a haunted look in her eyes. She could love this man if she wasn't careful. When she'd first met Peter in high school, she'd known they would marry.

She shook the thoughts from her mind. She'd just met Liam last week.

She grabbed her first-aid supplies and hurried to the backyard.

When she stepped onto the deck, Nana was talking with Liam. Next to Katie, Madison jumped to her feet.

"You are such a baby. How can you be so stupid?" Madison screamed, her hands clenched at her sides.

"No, I'm not," Katie yelled back, tears streaming down her face.

Liam turned toward Madison. "Maybe it's time for us to go."

Madison glared at her uncle. "I hate you all." She ran toward the gate.

Sarah tried to stop her, but she didn't move fast enough. "I'll go get her."

Halfway across the yard, Liam said, "It's my problem. I'll find her."

As he passed her she touched his arm and whispered, "I'll calm Katie down."

"I appreciate it. Right now I don't know what else to do for Madison."

The defeat in his voice tore at her heart. She cupped his hand and looked into his sad eyes. "Love her and be there for her like our Lord is for us. Be the father she needs."

He squeezed her hand then continued his trek toward the gate.

Sarah sent up a prayer for Liam. *He needs You, God. Help him say the right words to Madison.*

As Sarah joined Katie, still sobbing, Nana held four kittens in her lap with Gabe sitting in front of her. Katie had Blackie cradled against her chest.

Sarah sat cross-legged on the ground next to the little girl and put her arm around her shoulders. She didn't say anything as Katie struggled to stop crying.

"She's mean," the child said between sniffles. "I wish I didn't have a sister."

"You know, I always wanted a sister. It got kinda lonely being an only child. I had to play by myself a lot."

"Yeah, we used to play together all the time."

"What happened?"

Katie shrugged. "She's always mad now."

"What about you?"

"At her."

"Anyone else?"

Katie tilted her head toward Sarah, her forehead wrinkled. "This boy at school. He teases me on the playground."

"Why are you mad at her? Anything else besides yelling at you today?"

"She's always telling me I'm stupid." Katie lifted her chin. "I'm not stupid."

"No, you aren't. When a person is mad, she sometimes will say things she doesn't mean to someone she loves."

"But why?"

"Because she's upset about something."

"Daddy?"

"Maybe."

"She cries about him, especially at night."

"Have you told your uncle about that?"

Katie shook her head. "She'll get more mad at me."

"Why don't you try this? When Madison gets mad at you, ask Jesus to help her."

"Will He?"

"Yes. He doesn't like seeing people hurting."

Katie grinned and cuddled against Sarah, whose heart swelled at the warmth from this sweet girl. In that moment Sarah realized how much Katie and Madison meant to her.

In front of Sarah's house, Liam looked up and down the street. Where would Madison go when she was upset? Home? Aunt Betty's?

Then he remembered a place at the park she'd discovered on Monday while putting up posters and thought would be a perfect fort to play in. He would check there first then the other two places.

Five minutes later he spied the large shrubbery and jogged toward it. When he reached it, he knelt and stuck his head through the opening. Madison huddled in a corner, her legs drawn up and clasped against her chest.

"Go away."

"No."

"I'm not gonna talk to you." She set her mouth in a stubborn line he knew all too well.

"That's okay." Liam crawled under the vegetation, perfect for kids to fit through, not so much for a man six foot four. He hunched his shoulders and settled in the widest space across from Madison.

She laid her head on her knees and peered away for five minutes before she straightened and gave him a glare. "Ever since you came, my life has been—" tears welled in her eyes "—awful. Daddy's gone. Everything is different."

Liam sighed. Madison admitting this out loud was a step in the right direction. Usually she told him he wasn't her father and stomped away. And each time his own grief over his brother's death pierced his heart as it did Madison's.

"I know how you feel."

"How? You aren't me."

"Since I got the call about his death, my life has changed. Your daddy was my brother. I loved him very much. When we were kids, he was my best friend. He was only a couple of years younger—like you and Katie."

Madison chewed on her bottom lip. "She could have hurt herself bad today or…" She swiveled her head to stare through the branches.

"Were you worried she'd die?"

She nodded but wouldn't look at him.

Then he saw the tear roll down her cheek. "I imagine that was the way your dad felt when I knocked myself out doing tricks on my skateboard at the park. Good thing he saw me. He ran and got help like you did today with Katie."

She peered at him. "You should have been watching her better."

"You might be right, but no parent can be with a child all the time."

"You're not a parent."

Although the words hurt, he chose to ignore them and continued. "There comes a time a child has to make good choices. Think of the consequences of her actions. Like today, you hurt your sister's feelings because you took your anger out on her."

She started to protest, but he held up his hand, palm outward.

"Fear can drive a lot of emotions, especially anger. Once my dad told me that yelling at Gareth because he'd done something dumb wasn't going to solve the problem. He asked me instead to be an example for my younger brother. I tried, and we became closer. When either one of us had a problem, we knew the other would be there to listen. Sometimes that's all a person needs to know—that someone cares enough to listen to her problems."

"I listen all the time to Katie."

"Good. Have you shared your problems with her? It works both ways."

"She's six. What problems?"

"Age has nothing to do with it. Everyone has them. It's the relationship between you that counts. She loves you. That's why today she was so upset when you yelled at her. You hurt her. I have a feeling she already realized there was a better way to deal with Blackie than her climbing the tree."

She frowned. "Maybe."

"My dad told me that day that because I

was the oldest, I had to be the one to show my younger brother what was right."

Madison blew out a large breath and set her chin on her knees as she stared at the ground between them. "I wish everything was the same. I miss Daddy."

"I do, too."

Silence hovered between them. Liam wasn't sure what else he could say to make a difference.

Finally she lifted her head. "I'm sorry."

"Tell your sister that and why you were upset. Share your problems with her."

"Maybe."

"Are you ready to go back to Sarah's?"

She nodded and crawled toward the opening.

Liam followed her out, stood and dusted off his pants. "I see what you mean about this being a great fort. Your dad and I had a tree house. We spent a lot of time up there, playing and talking."

Halfway back to Sarah's house, Madison looked up at him. "Why doesn't Katie miss Daddy like I do?"

"Maybe she does. People mourn in different ways."

"Why did God take my daddy away?"

How do I answer her, Lord? I asked You that very question.

"I don't know, Madison. It was his time, and he's with the Lord now, keeping an eye on you. He loves you very much. That won't ever change." As he said that to Madison, he'd been talking about his brother but realized the words also applied to God.

When they arrived at Sarah's, Liam headed for the backyard. "We need to go home."

"Can I say goodbye to the kittens and Gabe first?"

"Sure. I'll give you time to do that."

Madison was the first through the gate and raced toward her sister, Sarah and Nana. When she hugged Katie, Liam thanked the Lord for the right words to say to Madison. Hope that things would become better for them as a family took root.

Sarah met him, smiling. "Whatever you said to Madison worked. She apologized to Katie."

"I told her about her father and me. We went through a rough patch growing up, and I passed on my father's advice to me. She didn't know her grandfather, but I'm sure Gareth talked about him all the time. He seemed to have the right advice when it was needed. That's what I remembered when I found Madison."

"Where did she go?"

"Under some big bushes at the park."

"And you knew where she was. That's wonderful, since I doubt it was obvious she was there."

For once in a long time he didn't feel alone. The Lord had been with him today but also Sarah. He took her hand and faced her. "Thank you for being here and understanding about the girls."

"Anytime. We all need help occasionally."

"Speaking of help, do you need me to come early tomorrow to help you get ready for the committee and maybe get on the same page about what we want to do for the fund-raiser?"

She chuckled. "Pastor Collins is great at railroading someone to do a task."

"You don't think your mom got to him, too?"

"I suppose so, but if he made the suggestion for us to be on the committee, it was because he felt we would be good. Pastor Collins has resisted my mom's ideas before because he didn't agree."

"Speaking of your mother, she just opened the kitchen door. That's my cue to get the girls and go home."

Sarah settled her hands at her waist. "While I'm stuck here. Thanks." Then she started laughing.

Liam waved toward Tina, rounded up his girls, told Nana goodbye and hurried out of the backyard before Sarah's mother had them doing something else together—not that it was a bad idea, but he hated being manipulated. His ex-wife had been great at it. The very thought of her ought to dampen any romantic feelings he had toward Sarah.

All they could be was friends. Good friends.

Chapter Seven

On Thursday night Sarah sat next to Liam on her couch while Pastor Collins wrapped up the first planning committee meeting for the fund-raiser. The whole evening she'd been aware of the man who was beside her. His scent—a woody floral smell—had teased her senses all evening. His casual touch when shifting on the cushion kept pulling her attention away from the topic of discussion.

"So we'll get together again in a couple of weeks after we've met with our individual committees. You'll have the people who sign up for your committees after this Tuesday's lunch meeting. Please meet with them in a week's time, so at the luncheon on the following Tuesday we can make sure everything is on track. Okay?" Pastor Collins's gaze skimmed the faces of each of the seven people in Sarah's living room, receiving a nod from everyone. "Let's close with a prayer."

Sarah bowed her head while the pastor thanked God for the group of volunteers.

Pastor Collins ended by saying, "Bless each one as they proceed forward to make this the biggest fund-raiser for the children in our town who need assistance. Amen."

Beatrice shot to her feet, her purse hugged against her chest. She was on the publicity committee with the pastor and had wanted to be in charge of the silent auction. But Brandon and Abigail Johnson were heading up that one. Beatrice said something to Pastor Collins then swung around and charged toward the front door before Sarah could move to the entry hall to say goodbye to everyone as they left.

After Abigail and two other members left, Pastor Collins approached Sarah. "Thanks for opening your home to us. I was pleasantly surprised we had snacks at the meeting. I especially enjoyed the stuffed mushrooms."

"Liam brought them along with the vegetable tray with the spinach artichoke dip. Mom made the rest."

"Liam's quite a cook. He went to check on the kids. Please tell him I appreciate the food. I've already thanked your mother."

"I will."

When she shut the front door, she went in search of the kids, still outside although it was dark now. The laughter from the back drew her. When she stepped onto the deck, the floodlights illuminated nearly half the yard. The four kids sat on the wooden planks playing with the kittens while Brandon entertained them with a story. Nana perched in a chair at the end of the circle of children while Liam stood with her mom by the railing.

Sarah circumvented Brandon and the kids to rescue Liam from her mother. No telling what she'd said in the ten minutes Sarah had let the other committee members out the front.

"I appreciate you writing down that stuffed mushroom recipe. They were delicious. Even the children ate them."

"That's why I fix it. Both my girls love them, and they don't realize how healthy they are. But I must say Madison has been on a healthy kick for the past month. If only Katie would be," he said with a long sigh. He caught sight of Sarah, something akin to relief flitting across his face. "Has everyone gone?"

"Yes, and Pastor Collins wanted me to thank you for the food, especially the stuffed mushrooms. They were a big hit with everyone." She shifted her gaze to her mom. "How were the kids?"

"Great. And after seeing Mama with the white kitten, I'm calling the allergist tomorrow. She hasn't put it down the whole evening. Thankfully there were four others. One for each child. As long as I kept my distance from the kittens, I was okay."

"Did Gabe get any attention?" Sarah spied him plopped down next to Katie.

"Both Katie and Seth threw the ball for him until I think he was exhausted. He hasn't moved from Katie's side for the past fifteen minutes."

"And that's why you never set up your campsite in a dried-up streambed unless you want to wake up the next morning in the middle of water, and in my case it hadn't even rained where we were. But it did upstream somewhere." Brandon pushed to his feet. "It's time we go home, boys. Tomorrow is a school day."

As Sarah's mother showed Brandon and his sons out, Madison joined Liam and Sarah. "Can we put the kittens in the shed for you?"

"Sure. I have a feeling they're ready to sleep after all this attention." When Madison left them, Sarah said to Liam, "You may have a problem. Katie is really attached to Blackie and Madison likes that calico cat she's been holding."

"Yeah, I see. Are you telling me we'll need to take both?"

"It would be fewer problems for you. I have that lady coming this Sunday for one of them. I don't want to give away any kitten they want."

"So I need to decide if I'm going to take one or two by Sunday?"

Sarah nodded, keeping her eye on the two girls as they carried two kittens each and Nana followed with hers. "If you have a chance to talk with Brandon tomorrow at work, let him know that I have at least one kitty left."

"I will, and I'll talk with the girls Saturday about them. I was thinking of setting up something in the utility room for when I'm working. After they've adjusted to our house, then I might leave them to roam the whole place but not at first."

"So you're not asking Betty to come over and check on them?"

"No. She already does so much for us. If the girls bond with their kittens, it might help them adjust to a move to Dallas."

Dallas? "You're moving. When?"

"From the beginning I'd planned to return to Dallas when the girls were doing better. I told my captain I hoped to be back before the end of this year. I have a house there and have only rented it out. The lease will be up at the end of October."

"So you don't see yourself living in Buffalo?" It took all her willpower to keep any disappointment out of her voice. But she was.

"I grew up in Dallas. Still have cousins who live there. I love the area."

"And Buffalo is very different from Dallas."

"Please don't say anything to Madison and Katie about moving. Nothing is settled, and I don't want them to worry about something that might or might not happen in the future."

Sarah latched on to the word "might." She didn't want to see him and his nieces leave. She enjoyed his and the girls' company. "I won't. It's not my place, and I won't say anything to Mom or Nana, either. They can never keep a secret."

"That's why I haven't said anything to Aunt Betty." He glanced toward the shed. "I was able to change my work schedule to have April 23 off for Madison's birthday."

"Great, but you might not be too excited with what I've come up with for her party."

His eyebrows scrunched. "What?"

"I remember one of the few parties my mother did for me was at the salon. The girls Madison invites will get an afternoon getting their nails done, their hair fixed and dressing up. Then a limousine will pick them up to go to dinner. I have a friend in Tulsa who did it for her daughter and sometimes does it for other little girls. It's called Princess for a Day. She's letting me borrow the fancy clothes from her."

"Where do I fit in with that?"

"You can run the selfie booth where they can pose for different pictures with their friends. My friend said I could borrow that, too. The booth is fun to have at parties. There are different backgrounds they can use."

"You came up with all that in a few days? But wouldn't you have to close down the salon to do that?"

"For the afternoon. But if this works, Mom and I can offer this for others, and I'll purchase the supplies like my friend did. Hopefully it will be a win-win for us."

He grinned, again slanting a look toward the shed. "You're a lifesaver. I don't know how she'll feel, but it'll be different."

"Trust me. Little girls love dressing up."

He moved close and cupped her face. "I do trust you. If you ever need help with anything, just ask. I'm a pretty good cook and handyman."

"All I need is for you to pay for the food and rent a limousine for the evening."

"Thank you, Sarah." His gaze snared hers.

And for the life of her she couldn't look away. Slowly he lowered his head and brushed his lips across hers before deepening the kiss.

For a brief moment she felt like a princess herself and her prince charming had bestowed a kiss on her. Until she heard giggles coming from the backyard.

She quickly stepped back at the same time Liam did. His face reddened. Hers did, too.

"We're going to hear about this for weeks," Sarah muttered and turned toward the two kids, her mom and grandmother coming toward the deck.

"Yep. I'll try to set the girls straight."

"And I will with my mother, but most likely she won't hear a word I say."

While the foursome ascended the stairs, he whispered, "Can I tell Madison about it? What is the limit on the number of girls she can invite?"

"Five besides Madison and Katie. Any more and it becomes too hectic. And, yes, tell her. It's only a little over two weeks away."

"Why don't you come with me, Madison and Katie?" her mother asked the girls. "I'll fix you a goodie bag to take home with you tonight. I love baking but have too many cookies to eat by myself. You two will be helping me."

Mom winked at Sarah as she guided Nana and the girls to the back door. "Maybe I'll sleep in the shed tonight. She's probably planning my wedding right now."

He chuckled.

"You wait. You have a long walk home with little girls with a hundred questions running through their minds."

"Oh. Right." He tried to wipe the grin off his face, but it leaked through. "We need to find a time to talk before the meeting next Tuesday. I'm freaking out inside. I've never done anything remotely like plan a bachelor auction."

"How about Sunday after church in the early afternoon at *your* house?"

"The girls are going to want to see the kittens and Gabe."

"I'll bring them to you. If you come over, it'll just fuel the fires of my mother's vivid imagination."

"Then it's a date." He started for the back door, stopped and whirled around. "I mean, not a *date* date. Just a good time to figure out what we're going to do."

The word *date* still rang through her mind. It took her a few seconds to respond. "I know." But as she said that, she actually wished it had been a real date. Disappointment wormed its way into her thoughts. What was happening to her?

After discussing the fund-raiser for an hour, Liam kneaded the knots in his neck and shoulders. He rose from his kitchen table that afforded him and Sarah a view of the backyard where the girls were playing with the dog and the kittens. "I'll contact the woman who ran the bachelor auction in Dallas and make sure we're doing everything we need to." He walked the stiffness out as he prowled the room. "I hope we can find twenty men to be in the auction. I'm glad you know a lot of people in town. My contacts are limited to firefighters, police officers and medical staff."

"How about the guys in the Single Dads' Club? Brandon would be great."

"So would Colt Remington and Michael Taylor. I'll check with them."

"See, that's a great start." Sarah stood and stretched.

"What if they say no?"

"It's for charity and for fun. So how about you?"

Liam stopped dead in his tracks and looked at Sarah. "Me?"

She closed the space between them. "Yes, you. Your friends will be more willing to participate if you do. Having a man cook for you is romantic."

He cocked a grin. "You're just saying that so I'll ask you to stay for dinner."

"Yes, but it's true. I want Mom asleep when

I return home tonight, or she'll give me the third degree."

"What did she say when you gathered up the animals and left?"

"She helped me put the kittens in the carrier. She's had one allergy shot, but it'll take a while before she can really be around a cat, if even then. She sneezed once."

Sarah's sweet, flowery scent flirted with his senses. He remembered their shared kiss and had to fight the urge to do it again. He had no business getting involved with anyone. He'd be leaving town in five or six months. Since his talk with Madison a few days ago, his relationship with her had improved. It gave him hope he'd be able to return to his hometown... and yet he'd miss Sarah. A lot. After the fundraiser was over and the girls had their own pets, he could back off and distance himself from Sarah. But that wasn't until June.

"I'm not sure what I should do for the kitten Nana is so attached to when his littermates are gone. He can't live in the shed by himself. I don't want to give him away if the shots will work for Mom. When Nana is home, that's all she does, play with the kitten she has named Junior."

"Are you sure it's a male?"

"No. It's not easy to tell, but I think it is. I

have an appointment with the vet tomorrow for all five kittens. I'll know more then."

"I'd be interested in what sex the two kittens the girls want are." He walked to the window to check on his nieces and count all the animals. He didn't want a repeat of last Wednesday.

"So you've decided you're taking two of them?"

As he watched Madison and Katie playing with the kittens, he made a decision. "Yes. I'm hoping it will teach them responsibility. I've made it clear they'll need to care for them."

"That leaves only one kitty to find a home for. Did Brandon say anything to you about Seth and Jared taking one?"

"He said no. The boys have their heart set on a dog. But he doesn't want to do it until he puts up a fence. I told him I would help."

"I think, then, I'll pay your aunt a visit tomorrow after I see the vet. She showed some interest. Like with Nana, I think it'll help Betty. Caring for a pet will be good for her, especially when the girls aren't around."

And that might not be for long. But he wasn't going to tell Aunt Betty for a while, not until he was ready to talk with his nieces. He wanted them to hear it from him. He'd be glad when his life was more settled. This past half year had been disruptive to a man who liked to have a schedule. Little was in his control.

"However it's supposed to work, it will."

He hoped Sarah was right about that. "Since no one came forward about the lost kittens, if you hadn't taken them in, no telling what would have happened to them."

She came up behind him and stood next to him, looking out at the girls. "I think they ended up in my yard for a reason. Somehow I think Nana will be able to keep Junior. She isn't really working much at the salon so this will give her something to do. According to my mother, when Nana physically couldn't stand for more than ten or fifteen minutes at a time and she quit taking clients, she went downhill fast. I think she's bored. Yes, she is forgetting things, but she seems depressed to me since I came home. Mom doesn't see it since it's happened gradually. She's enjoyed the times the girls are at our house. That's why we came home early yesterday so she could see them."

"Yeah, I noticed they talked a lot to Nana. She's been telling them about her cat Sammy." He glanced at Sarah. "I think we've done about all we can until our whole committee meets Tuesday at the luncheon. I'm going to tell Madison and Katie they need to pick their two kittens from the three not spoken for."

"Good idea. Do you have the utility room fixed up yet?" She trailed behind him out the back door.

"No, and I probably should get it done today. Tuesday before I pick up the girls at school will be busy."

"I'll go with you and show you what I'm using. If they have the same litter and food, the transition will be easier."

"Sure, we can go right now if you want."

"Sounds good. I have an idea. Is your aunt home?"

"Yes." He slowed his pace then stopped before reaching his nieces. "What are you plotting?"

She laughed. "I've never been good at hiding what I'm thinking. I'm going to see if Betty would like to meet the kitten I have left to be adopted. If so, she could stay with the girls out here while we run to the store. I figure if she doesn't fall in love with the kitten by the time we come back, then I need to look for a home for it."

"I don't know. She's going to have the kids tomorrow."

"Then she'll say no. I still want her to see the kitten. And you're not doing the asking. I am."

He turned his back on his nieces and leaned close. "And shopping with two little girls can test the best of men. I always walk out with more than I intended to buy. Some I didn't even realize were in the basket."

"That can be a challenge." She began to move toward the girls but stopped, looking up at him. "You're doing a good job. This time next year things will be different, more settled. Any change takes time. Even when I moved back to Buffalo, I had to adjust, and this was my hometown."

Outside Liam joined his nieces, who had built a cardboard maze for the kittens and squatted to peek into the opening. Katie lay on her back with two kitties climbing all over her. One was playing with her long hair. Her giggles floated to him. Madison held the other kittens while Gabe stretched out beside her. She moved from one animal to the next, petting each of them.

Liam sat beside her on the ground. "If you could have a kitten, which one would you pick?"

"Buffy." She pointed at the one she cradled in her lap.

"Buffy? How did you come up with that name?"

"After Buffalo. I live in the best town, but the full name was too much. Buffy fits her the best."

"So you think she's a girl?"

"That's what Sarah thinks." She glanced toward Sarah crossing through Aunt Betty's yard. "I like her. How about you?" She slanted a look at him.

More than he should. It wasn't easy keeping his feelings in check with someone like Sarah—so different from his ex-wife. "Yep, she's a nice lady."

"Will I get to keep Buffy? Katie wants Blackie."

"It would be tough to have to choose between those two. What do you think we should do?"

"Keep both?" Madison hugged Buffy against her chest.

"I like that suggestion. Sarah said we can bring them here on Tuesday after she takes them to the vet tomorrow."

"We can!" Madison hopped to her feet and raced for the cardboard maze. "Katie, we get to keep both!" She disappeared inside while her sister squealed.

As Aunt Betty and Sarah headed toward Liam, Madison and Katie crawled out, each holding two cats, the biggest grins on their faces. Both charged across the yard and skidded to a halt in Sarah's path.

Liam watched them tell Sarah how excited

they were while petting Gabe. "Hopefully things around your house will get back to normal soon. Most of your little guests will be gone." Gabe cocked his head at Liam, the Lab's big brown eyes staring up at him. "But what's normal anymore?"

"Whatever the day brings," Sarah said, suddenly stepping in front of him.

"Live for the present?"

"It's the only way to keep from losing your sanity, or at least I've been told."

"Who?"

"Pastor Collins when I first returned to Buffalo. Worrying about the future is pointless and a waste of time and the past is over with and done. You can't have do overs, so why dwell on it?" Sarah knelt next to Gabe, giving him a hug.

"Good advice but hard to follow."

"Why do you say that?"

"The past is what makes me who I am. My victories. My defeats."

"True, but ultimately you decide who you are. You define yourself, not your past. That's something we actually can control."

"I wish it was that easy."

"I never said it was easy. There are things in my past that I'm still trying to work through."

"Your husband's death?"

"Yes. I didn't realize how much coming home would bring up my memories."

Katie hurried up to them. "Aunt Betty is taking a kitten!"

"That's great. Now all of them will have a home."

Liam hadn't lost a spouse to death but to divorce. Dreams died that day. In his own way, he understood what Sarah was going through.

His youngest niece threw her arms around his neck and kissed his cheek then did the same to Sarah. "I can't wait until Tuesday. Blackie and me have been making plans. She's gonna sleep with me." Then Katie dashed back to her sister and aunt.

"Speaking of sleeping, we need to go to the store. Betty said she could stay here while we go if we'll also pick up some for her. She's going to take her kitten tonight." Sarah shoved to her feet. "Ready?" she asked as they headed for his car.

As Liam drove toward the supercenter, he asked, "What are you going to do about Nana's kitten on Tuesday when all the others are gone?"

"He's still too young to roam free. I wouldn't want him to get lost or hurt. I'm not sure what to do. I still want to see if it will work with Nana keeping him."

Liam pulled into a parking space at the store, switched off the engine then shifted toward Sarah. "Since the other day when we talked, I've been thinking about it. I could temporarily take the kitten until you find a solution or, if not, another home for him. Your grandmother can visit with him anytime and maybe do some trial runs to see how the medication and shots work for your mother."

"When he gets older, he can spend more time outside. I've been reading up on it. Sometimes restricting where the cat can be in a house helps and also restricting my mother's contact with him could help. Are you sure?"

"If I don't take him temporarily, you'll need to find a home for him until he's old enough to be an outside cat. So, yes, I'm sure. Friends help each other." He wanted more than friendship with Sarah, and that troubled him. "You don't think a dog would work better for your grandmother?"

"She pets Gabe, but it isn't the same. The cat is a connection to her past."

Liam opened the door. "All we can do is try it. If it doesn't work, you aren't any worse off."

"I promise I'll have a solution in a couple of months. And if for some reason Nana loses interest, then I can find a home. I can think of a few ladies who get their hair done at the salon who might be interested."

Liam waited for Sarah to get out and then they walked toward the store together. When their arms brushed against each other, he took her hand. She made him feel less alone in the world. Between Sarah and the Single Dads' Club, for the first time he thought everything would work out with him and his nieces.

Chapter Eight

❧

Liam sat on the bottom bleacher in the pool area at Buffalo High School. Madison and Katie were in the swimming class, and Britney Simmons was showing six girls how to do the breaststroke. Sarah helped the teacher as each student swam across the shallow end, practicing what had been demonstrated. Madison mastered it right away while Katie struggled, stopping halfway then restarting with Sarah's assistance. At the end of their time, Britney had them float on their backs, teaching them to relax.

Liam appreciated Sarah making sure his nieces got into a class where she was helping the teacher. When both of them heard Sarah would be there, too, they were excited. And, even though Katie was a little scared of the water, with Sarah there she'd gone right into the pool.

Every time he saw Sarah with Madison and Katie, he wondered if they could have a relationship beyond friendship. Madison and Katie needed a woman's touch—even Gareth had told him that on more than one occasion.

As the class exited the water, Liam shook away his thought of having more with Sarah. There was so much working against them. He needed to accept what wasn't going to be, to relish the time he would have with her and return to Dallas by the end of the year.

"Did you see me, Uncle Liam? I almost swam across the pool. Next time I will." Katie grabbed her beach towel and wrapped it around her while Madison was talking with Sarah near the pool.

"You did a great job. This is only the first lesson. Wait until the next one. You'll be going everywhere."

"Even in the deep end?"

"Yes, if you can swim, but you do know you never swim alone."

"Miss Britney said that to us. There should always be an adult around who knows how to swim. Do you, Uncle Liam?"

"Yes, I helped your daddy learn how."

Katie swept around and settled one hand

on her waist. "C'mon, Madison. Blackie and Buffy will get lonely their first night at our house."

Her older sister stuck her tongue out at Katie. "Hold your horses." Madison flounced toward them.

"I don't have any horses. I have a kitten waiting for me to come home." Katie poked her tongue out then turned her back on her sister.

Madison had been much better lately, but Liam prepared himself for one of her outbursts. He glanced at Sarah at the side of the pool, watching them, trying not to laugh.

Madison stopped in front of Liam. "I asked Sarah if she would let us ride with her on Thursday. She said yes. You'll be working. Can we?"

"The time to ask if you can was before you asked her. Aunt Betty is bringing you. It's all arranged."

"But—"

Before Madison worked herself up, he added, "Besides, Sarah has another class after this one. See, the boys are coming in."

"I told Sarah Katie and me could watch the boys' class. We might learn something."

He started to give her a flat-out no, but then he thought instead he would first talk to Sarah. Aunt Betty hated to drive when it was getting dark. "I'll think about it."

"Thanks, Uncle Liam. You'll see, it'll be okay." Madison dug into the bag and pulled out her towel to dry off. "The next class doesn't start for ten minutes. Katie and me can wait here."

In other words he should go talk to her now. Otherwise they probably wouldn't see each other until Monday when they were getting together to compare notes about the bachelor auction before the meeting that evening. He headed toward her.

Sarah came halfway to the end of the bleachers. "I have no problem with taking them on Thursday and the other times you're working."

"Don't you have two classes before this one? Madison may think she and Katie will sit watching the one after theirs, but not through the two before. It's light enough at six thirty that I think Aunt Betty will be okay with bringing them. At least she said she would." Liam pictured the lines of tension in his aunt's face as she'd agreed. "But it would be great if you could take them home afterward. Is that all right?"

"You're becoming quite the diplomat. That should make both Madison and Aunt Betty happy."

"It's a necessity for a parent. I'm learning I have to pick my battles with the girls."

"Not bad advice to follow in everything."

"I thought Colt was bringing his daughter Beth for swimming lessons in their class."

"Britney told me one of his horses became ill and he was waiting for the vet to show up. Beth will be here on Thursday. Do your nieces know her?"

"Yes, through the single dads' group."

"Good. She'll know some of the girls." Sarah glanced at a couple of the boys jumping into the pool. "That's my signal class is about to start. See you later."

The smile that she threw him as she walked away lifted him, especially after a long day of trying to recruit a few firefighters and police officers to be bachelors in the auction.

"Let's go, girls." Liam motioned for Madison and Katie to leave.

His nieces hurried to him, still wrapped in their towels.

"I can't wait to get home and see Blackie. I hope she wasn't too lonely while we were gone." Katie raced ahead and exited first.

Madison quickly caught up with her. "At least they have each other. Poor Junior out in the shed by himself."

The house was only ten minutes away from the high school, but they made a brief stop at a local fast-food place to grab a quick dinner at the drive-through. As Liam pulled into their driveway, the porch light was on because it was almost dark. Liam punched the garage door opener.

"Look! Gabe is here!" Madison pointed toward the porch.

The Lab came to his feet, his tag wagging.

"Girls, hop out and keep Gabe on the porch while I park in the garage."

When he slid from the front seat, he headed for his nieces while retrieving his cell phone from his pocket. As he mounted the steps, he placed a call to Sarah and left a message, since she was still helping with the swimming lessons.

Madison and Katie flanked Gabe, who sat between them. His oldest niece held his collar, although he didn't think the Lab would run away. He had purposefully come here. But why?

"He's sad. He misses Blackie and Buffy." Katie stroked her hand down his long back. "Like we miss him and the other kittens."

"You've seen Aunt Betty's."

"She let us name her Sadie. That was the one I said." Madison straightened her shoulders and tilted her chin up.

Katie stopped petting Gabe and scooted around to face her sister. "Only cuz you said your name first. There was nuthin' wrong with Peppy."

"That's no name for a girl cat."

Before they started arguing he decided to try a technique one of the men in the single dads' group suggested—divert attention. "We need to get inside and check on your kittens. They'll be glad to see Gabe."

Both girls charged into the house, heading for the kitchen.

His cell phone rang. It was Sarah. "Gabe is fine. He's here."

"I can't believe he got out again. I thought we patched the fence. Obviously chicken wire didn't work. I'm leaving now. See you in a few minutes." Her exasperation rang clearly in her voice.

When Liam entered the kitchen and put the bag of hamburgers on the counter, Gabe lay on the floor with the kittens climbing on him. Katie was probably right. He missed his pals.

"See, Uncle Liam." His youngest niece pointed toward the Lab. "I could tell. His eyes were sad. Now he isn't. He should stay the night."

"Yeah, she's right. We should have a sleepover," Madison said to Gabe, but the words were for Liam.

This was a battle he would have to fight.

"Sarah is on her way to get him. Gabe is her dog. In time he'll forget about Blackie and Buffy."

Katie stuck her lower lip out. "No, he won't. And he won't forget us. He loves us."

"I agree. Gabe loves you all, but he still belongs to Sarah." He didn't want to get into an argument again over keeping the Lab. "We need to eat our dinner while we wait for Sarah to come. Go wash your hands."

Reluctantly they hurried to the downstairs bathroom while Liam set the food on the table. He managed to eat half of his burger before the doorbell rang. The girls jumped to their feet.

"Stay and finish eating. I'll answer the door."

Sarah had gone by her house first and, sure enough, Gabe had destroyed the chicken wire over the hole in the fence. She'd made sure that Junior was safely in the shed then walked over to Liam's with her leash.

When the door swung open, a frustrated Liam stood in the entrance. "Prepare yourself. The girls want Gabe to spend the night."

"I realize Gabe knows where your house is, but why did he come here?"

"Katie thinks he missed the kittens."

Sarah came into the entry hall and faced

him. "Even more reason not to let him stay. I can't reinforce Gabe getting out and going where he wants." The last time she went through three days of anguish wondering where Gabe was. She wasn't going to lose him if she could help it.

"I totally agree with you. In fact, if you want, I'll come down tomorrow and see if I can fix the fence while the kids are at school."

"What needs to be done most likely is to replace the boards. If you have to buy any supplies, I'll reimburse you their cost. There are about ten rotten boards at the bottom. Our run-off water flows through there."

"No problem. I'll take a look and take care of fixing the fence. I have a stake in this, too. Every time Gabe comes here, I become the bad guy to my nieces."

"Let's change that tonight. I'll firmly let them know Gabe stays at my house. Where are the girls?"

"In the kitchen finishing their dinner."

Sarah made her way down the hall. She could never explain how important Gabe was to her without telling Madison and Katie about losing her unborn child and husband. And that was something they didn't need to know. They were still dealing with their father's death. She didn't like talking about the miscarriage because, deep down, she still felt she could have avoided it if she'd paid more attention. Her mother didn't even know how she felt. It was a secret she couldn't tell another, but the knowledge that things could have been vastly different plagued her.

"Sarah!" Both girls shouted at the same time.

Madison dropped her last bite of hamburger and hurried to her. "Gabe is all right. We've been taking good care of him."

Katie tried to wheedle between her sister and Sarah. "He's happy now that he sees Blackie and Buffy."

With a smile Sarah clasped each one's shoulder. "I never worry about him when he's with you." Then she called Gabe to her side. "I wish I could stay and talk more about what you thought of your first swimming lesson, but I need to take him home. I can't have him thinking he can run away anytime he wants and get rewarded by staying. Now that you have your own pets, you'll find out what I mean."

Her eyes wide, Katie shook her head. "No, I won't ever let Blackie run away."

"Me, too, with Buffy." Madison held her kitten against her chest, petting it.

"Those kittens have very special owners. See

you Thursday at swimming." Sarah hugged Madison and Katie then started for the hallway.

"Uncle Liam needs a hug, too," Katie called out.

Heat suffused Sarah's face as she slowly looked toward Liam. She gave him a quick embrace, the whole time thinking of the kiss he'd given her. "Bye."

As she hurried toward the entryway, Liam wasn't far behind her. She kept her head forward, her cheeks still flaming. At the front door she turned around, one hand gripping the knob. "I shouldn't have done that."

He closed the space between them. "I'm glad you did. I can always use a hug. It's been a difficult six months, and I have a feeling it has been hard for you since you came back to Buffalo. Am I right?" One eyebrow lifted.

She gave him a nod then grappled with opening the door. Ten seconds later she scurried down the steps and, with Gabe by her side, rushed home before she went back to Liam, threw her arms around him again and kissed him. As she'd hugged him, she'd wanted more. She didn't deserve it. She'd survived the wreck while Peter and her baby died. Why hadn't she died?

What do You want me to do, Lord?

No answer formed in her mind. She was here and needed to do the best job she could.

As she approached her home, she saw it was all lit up. Was something wrong? Mom rarely had that many lights on. Sarah quickened her pace and let herself into the house by the front door.

"Mama, is that you?" Her mom came from the living room, deep lines marking her face in worry and exhaustion. Her brows scrunched together and her eyes darkened. "Nana isn't in her bedroom. I've looked everywhere and I can't find her."

"The door was locked when I came in. Did she leave her purse in her room?"

"Yes."

"Let's check to see if her keys are in it." Tightness expanded in Sarah's chest as she hastened to Nana's bedroom. She looked in her grandmother's bag that went everywhere with her. As Sarah dug around in it, her fingers clasped the keys at the bottom, and she held them up. "Then she should be here or…she's in the garage or in the backyard. We should search there first."

"I'll look in the garage and the cars." Her mom made her way toward the kitchen.

"I'll be out back."

When Sarah came outside, she paused and

scanned the yard. The bright floodlight on the deck illuminated many dark crevices but not all. Her gaze fell on the shed, a slither of light peeking out from under its door. She'd turned it off when she put Junior in there for the night. She'd had to listen to his whines as she walked away. She'd needed to go get Gabe at Liam's, but she'd intended to come back and play with Junior and her Lab for a while.

Hoping her grandmother was in there, she marched toward the shed. When she opened the door, she found Nana in a lounge chair, the white kitty curled in her lap on top of the blanket covering her grandmother. Her eyelids were half closed, but as Sarah crossed to her, they popped open wide.

"Oh, dear, what time is it? Is it morning?" Then Nana peeked around Sarah, her forehead creases deepening. "It's dark."

"Why are you out here? You scared Mom and me. We didn't know where you were." The day had been long and with two hours of swimming and having to retrieve Gabe, weariness had spread through Sarah like a neglected garden being overrun with weeds.

"Junior was crying. I couldn't stand to hear it. I decided to sleep out here. I can't leave him alone. He misses his sisters."

"Remember he has to stay out here because Mom is allergic to cats."

"Child, I remember that, but I still can't leave Junior by himself. It's not fun being lonely."

That last sentence struck a cord in Sarah. Ever since Peter died, emptiness had filled her heart. Even though she was around people all day, she was lonely in the crowd. Coming back to Buffalo had only amplified that feeling.

"Mama! You can't leave like that," Sarah's mother said from the doorway. Her hand over her chest, she continued. "I thought you went out and were wandering around lost." She stayed where she was, moving a step back.

Sarah shifted toward her mother. "Nana wants to sleep out here with Junior."

"No way. It still gets chilly at night."

"Tina, that's why I have a blanket. I'm not a child. I'm your mother. I can decide where I'm going to sleep. Junior needs me. He's a baby still."

"Mom, how about Nana bringing Junior in at bedtime and sleeping in her room with the door shut. Then in the morning, Nana, you can take him outside until we leave for work, then he can stay in the shed. Hopefully this is temporary. Let's try that for a night."

As her mother thought about what she'd said,

Sarah was encouraged because not once while standing in the doorway had Mom sneezed.

"Okay, but I won't be able to go into Mama's room to clean."

Nana pushed herself to her feet then scooped Junior into her arms. "I want to clean my own room. I'm not an invalid, so stop treating me like I am. If I need help in my room, Sarah is here." She walked out of the shed, head held high. "Sarah, bring the litter box and water bowl."

"Will do." Sarah hefted the box but left the pan. "I'll get something for water we can leave in her bedroom."

Mom fell into step with Sarah. "The allergy pills seem to be helping some…but what if this doesn't work?"

"Liam said he would take Junior until I found a home for him or your allergies are under control. If we don't, I don't see any way of getting Nana inside to sleep."

"Yeah, I know. She's a very determined woman. That part hasn't changed. While you set Nana up with Junior, I'll bring Gabe out here and keep an eye on him. We've got to re-think the fence."

"I've got that taken care of. Liam is going to replace the boards tomorrow."

"Wow. Liam is doing quite a bit for us. It's

nice having a young man around. Don't you think, Sarah?"

"Mom, I'm not answering you. I know where this is headed."

"You've been spending a lot of time with him and helping with a birthday party for Madison."

Sarah halted and set the litter box on the deck. "I'm spending a lot of time with him because you made sure I was on the fund-raising committee and he was, too. Did you also say something to Pastor Collins about us serving on a subcommittee together?"

"No, he came up with that all on his own. But it's interesting that he thinks you two would work well together."

Sarah rolled her eyes, let out a huff, picked up the litter box and hurried inside. Not only did she live in the same house as her mother, she worked side by side with her, too. They needed to talk after she set up Junior with Nana.

Lord, give me patience. Mom's driving me crazy, not Nana.

After settling Junior in Nana's room, Sarah found her mother in the kitchen heating water for hot tea. After fixing a cup of tea with lavender, Sarah sat at the table. "We need to have a talk."

Both of her mother's eyebrows shot up. "Oh, that sounds serious."

She needed her mother to understand why she wasn't looking for a husband. While Mom took the chair across from her, Sarah took a sip of the calming tea. "I don't want to get married again. At least for now. Liam and I are friends." As she said the last sentence the sensations that assailed her when they had kissed surged to the foreground.

"Friendship is a great basis for a marriage."

She and Peter had been best friends, but she was alive and he wasn't. "I know that but…" How did she tell her mother she couldn't shake her guilt that she was the only one who'd walked away from the wreck?

"You and Peter had a great marriage. Mine to your father caused me to doubt if I ever wanted to marry again, but you know what a good relationship is like. Don't you want that again?"

Sarah had put her whole heart into her marriage, but when Peter died her life had shattered. And she hadn't figured out how to put it back together.

"What's going on, Sarah? Anytime we start talking about the past, you clam up. Keeping things bottled up inside you isn't dealing with them. Burying them won't protect you from them."

Sarah's throat jammed with a knot of emotions ranging from anger that her mother wanted Sarah to talk to regret that she didn't know how to express what she was experiencing, especially since coming to Buffalo. "I shouldn't have come home. Too many memories."

"Are they good ones?"

"Usually."

"I know it's been hard for you to drive by the wreck site." Her mother reached across the table and covered her hand with hers. "Hon, I wish I could take your pain away, but that's something you have to do for yourself. I'm not saying forget the past, just move on from it. Peter would have wanted that for you. You've always wanted a family. That means finding a husband. You'd be a terrific mother. I've seen you with Madison and Katie. You're good for those girls. You will be for your own children, too."

The pressure in Sarah's chest expanded. "I was pregnant," she whispered in a raspy voice as she tried to drag enough oxygen into her lungs. "And I lost her." She couldn't continue talking with her mother. She bolted to her feet and hurried toward the hallway.

"Sarah, it's not like you to avoid a problem."

Her vision blurred, Sarah slowed her escape.

"I won't press you anymore, but I'm here if you need to talk. I know moving back here has been hard for you, but I'm glad you did. I need your help with Nana. Tonight proved that."

Sarah made it to her bedroom before the tears cascaded down her cheeks. She hadn't cried since she left Buffalo, but the sobs wouldn't stop. She had years' worth to release.

Chapter Nine

At the end of dinner at a steak house on Monday night with Madison, Liam lounged back in his chair. "When summer comes, I'd like to take you on an all-day outing someplace you'd like to go. So start thinking of what you and I can do together."

"The Tulsa Zoo. I went once when I was six. I'd love to go back."

"Perfect."

"Katie should like it, too."

"This trip will be for just you and me. I'll take Katie where she wants to go, even the Tulsa Zoo, but a different day. I want us to spend time together. So much has happened in the past six months. So, is there anything you want to ask me?"

"Do you like Sarah?"

"Yes, she's a good friend. Why? Don't you?"

"Yes." Madison shrugged. "I was just wondering. You two spend a lot of time together."

"We're working on the summer camp fundraiser. Did you ever go to it?"

"I loved the rodeo the year they had that, but I was too young to participate in it. You had to be at least eight. I hope you all do something like that."

So far this first solo outing to strengthen his relationship with his nieces was going all right. He was glad someone suggested it. "This year we're having an auction and dinner. I thought we would buy tickets and take Aunt Betty. What do you think?"

"What kind of dinner?"

"A dress-up one."

Her mouth contorted into an expression of distaste. "Yuck. Is Sarah coming, too?"

Both of his nieces would rather wear pants than a dress, so Madison had surprised him when she'd said that one of her favorite foods was steak and wanted to go to a steak restaurant. "She'll be there with her mom and grandmother."

Madison scanned the restaurant, every table set with fine china, silverware and elegant glasses on top of a white tablecloth. "Will it be fancy like this?"

"Not quite. It's going to be at church in the

large rec hall. If you don't want to go, some teenagers will be watching the children not attending."

"I'll check with my friends. I don't wanna be the only kid there."

His throat dry, Liam took a deep gulp of ice water. "How are you and Buffy getting along?"

She giggled. "When I woke up this morning, she was sitting on my chest. Her whiskers tickled my chin." Her expression sobered. "But I don't want to roll over on her and hurt her. Do you think she'll be all right?"

"She's feisty. She'll be able to take care of herself or let you know."

"Yeah, her whine is loud."

"Do you want any dessert?"

"Yes! Chocolate cake."

"That sounds good to me." He signaled their waiter. When the man appeared at the table, Liam ordered two slices of chocolate cake. "This young lady is having a birthday this coming Saturday."

Madison beamed. "I can't believe Sarah is having me and my friends at the salon. I've never had my hair fixed. She's so nice and always listens to me."

He cherished the sight of his niece's face lit up with enthusiasm. It had been a rough half year for them. He didn't want her birthday to pass her by without a big production. He'd lost both of his parents at different times and still felt their loss even after all these years. Gareth had been the last of his immediate family and now that he was gone, too, Liam wanted to make a family with his nieces. "I want you to have a great day. You only turn eight once."

"You're gonna miss my birthday. You work that day." Her grin fell.

"That's one of the things I wanted to tell you tonight. I traded Saturday with another guy at the fire station. I'll be working on Friday, but I'll be home Saturday morning to spend time with you celebrating." She didn't know about the limousine and plans after the salon. That was to be a surprise.

"You're gonna be at the salon?" Her voice sounded more curious than surprised.

"You don't think I can paint nails?"

She stared at him for a long moment then burst out laughing. "If you do, I'm taking a picture of it."

"You've got yourself a deal. I'll start with your fingernails."

Her giggles increased. Liam relished the sound.

When the waiter brought them cake, there

was a lit candle on one slice. "Happy birthday, miss."

Madison blushed, murmured a thank-you and dug into the chocolate cake as though she hadn't eaten a steak, French fries and salad beforehand. "I love chocolate." When she finished the dessert, she had some smeared at the corner of her mouth.

"You've got some here." He indicated the area on his face.

"I like this evening, especially the stories about my dad. I can't believe he stomped through your snow fort."

"Yep, but I pelted him with a shower of snowballs not long after that. He never did that again. It had taken me hours to build my fort. Mom had him help me rebuild the one he destroyed."

"I miss Daddy."

"I do, too. Not only was he my brother but a friend. Like you and Katie."

"But sometimes I like to do things without her."

"I remember feeling that way, too. That's why I want us to go out by ourselves a couple of times a month. You two don't always want to do the same thing. That's normal."

"Yeah, Katie wouldn't sit still here like I

have." Madison thrust back her shoulders. "She can be a baby at times."

After paying the bill Liam said, "We'd better go home. You still have school tomorrow."

"Are we going to camp this summer?"

"Yes."

"I think Aunt Betty gets tired having us."

"She still loves you both, but she doesn't have the energy she used to. Besides, I thought you might want to be around other kids."

"I do. A lot of my friends are going. It's just that Aunt Betty seems to be upset lately. Was it because we scared her when we went to see Gabe?"

"Maybe." Liam clasped her hand as they walked to the car.

"We aren't gonna do it again. But she's always with us, watching us like we are."

"Sometimes when a person is let down by someone, it takes a while to regain their trust."

He started the car then looked at Madison sitting in the backseat. "You and Katie will always have me. I love you and want us to be a family."

Silence greeted that declaration. After a few seconds Liam backed out of the parking space, hoping he hadn't blown it with Madison. She was trying to cling to her old life, and he couldn't blame the child. Change was hard, and she was learning that the difficult way.

* * *

Sarah settled on the steps to the deck as Katie played with Gabe, and Nana sat in a lounge chair holding Junior asleep in her lap. Liam's niece had been with both pets until her grandmother came outside, but tonight instead of taking the white kitten inside to her bedroom, she'd stayed and watched Katie.

"She's adorable," Sarah's mother said behind her and took a seat on the top stair. "You and Katie seemed to have fun cooking dinner."

"Don't get any ideas that I'll take over the cooking anytime soon. It was just sandwiches. I knew today was a long day for you." Sarah glanced over her shoulder at the dark circles under her mom's eyes.

"Beatrice was extra picky today. How's she been on the fund-raiser committee?"

"Tolerable. Thankfully, I'm not working directly with her. Between Liam and me, we almost have our twenty bachelors."

"Are they all young?"

Sarah shifted halfway around on the step. "Yes."

"You might want to throw in some older men."

"I hadn't thought about that. Any suggestions?"

"At church there's Clarence Dodd and Tom

Adkins. I image they'll turn a few women's heads."

This was a first. Her mom was a friend with both of them, but she'd never said something like that. "Anyone else?" She drew on her willpower to keep from smiling and probing further about the two men.

"I know what you're thinking. I'm not going to bid on either man but others might. Just saying you should think about it."

"Why won't you bid on them? You've always supported this fund-raiser."

"Because I'll concentrate on trying to spend my money at the silent auction." Her mom paused, looked in the direction of Nana and added, "The truth is, I don't have time to date. I need to be here for Mama."

"I'm here, too. I can help with that."

"I'd rather see you bid on a bachelor than me."

At the sound of the gate opening Katie whirled around and ran to Liam and Madison coming into the backyard. Not sure how to answer her mother, Sarah leaped to her feet and hurried over to the trio. How could she explain to her mom that she didn't want anyone else to bid on Liam when she didn't understand it herself?

"Did you two have fun?" Sarah asked, surprised her mother hadn't followed her to get an answer.

"I got a candle on my chocolate cake." Madison ran her tongue over her lips. "Mmm. It was great."

Katie tugged on Madison's arm. "You should see Junior. He's really growing. Nana thinks he's gonna be *big*."

As the two girls scurried to her grandmother sitting under the oak tree, Liam chuckled. "Did Katie behave herself this evening?"

"We made dinner. How are they doing cooking dinner for you?"

"Let's just say it's a work in progress. I'm doing most of the work, but they're learning, especially about cleaning as you go."

"That's good. I didn't when I was growing up because Mom loved to do it, and now I'm nearly helpless in the kitchen."

His eyes twinkled. "I don't see you helpless in any situation."

"Then you've never seen me cook." She peered at the girls. "Did it go well?"

"Yes. I think so. No angry words exchanged. She even told me all about what's going on at school without me asking."

"That's good. Katie said she can't wait until she goes out with you next Monday."

"Is it safe for me to approach your mom?"

"We had a talk last week about backing off. I guess all we can do is see." As she headed toward the deck she added, "I'm worried about her. I suggested to her about getting a caregiver support group started at church, but I don't think she's tried. I'm going to talk to Pastor Collins after the fund-raiser luncheon tomorrow. If she won't, I will."

"Good thinking. If there hadn't been a single dads' group already, I would have if someone had suggested it to me. You feel overwhelmed and starting anything new seems too much, even something that would help you."

She slowed her pace. "Nana had a spell today when Beatrice was there. And that woman told Mom again that she needs to check into nursing homes for my grandmother. That didn't sit well with my mother."

"Hasn't she been doing better lately?"

"Yes. I think the new meds have helped— and it really wasn't too bad today—but Beatrice doesn't know how to mind her own business. My mom doesn't need the added stress."

"You've done so much for me. If I can help, let me know. Maybe you and your mom could talk to Pastor Collins together. You could drop your grandmother and Junior off at my house. She might enjoy seeing the other kittens."

"Maybe I will next week. I'll call Pastor Collins and set up an appointment with him. Thanks." Just having a game plan made Sarah feel less tense about the situation with Nana.

When he reached the bottom of the steps, Liam grinned at her mom. "How's it going with your mother and Junior at night?"

"Not too bad, but I don't know if that kitten will ever see the rest of the house." Her mother started to stand but sank back down.

When he offered her his hand, he helped her to stand. "I'm learning the importance of compromise with my nieces," he told her, smiling.

"I have some cookies left over from my baking yesterday. I'm going to wrap up some for you to take home." Her mother walked into the house.

"I vacuum Nana's bedroom several times a week," Sarah told him as the door closed behind her mother. "My grandmother has taken to eating in her bedroom in the morning, so she can spend more time with Junior. In the evening if it's not raining, she's outside. Both Gabe and Junior like that. It won't be long before the kitten tries to climb the fence to see what's on the other side."

"Has Gabe gotten out anymore since I fixed the fence?"

"No. I saw him once try, though. I don't

want to leave him inside all day. He loves the outdoors." The urge to kiss Liam for the work he'd done last Wednesday inundated her. These past weeks she'd enjoyed his company as well as the girls. With Liam down the street, she didn't feel so alone. She'd lost touch with a lot of her friends since she'd moved away. He'd filled a void she hadn't realized until he came into her life.

"Have you thought of getting a GPS tracker for Gabe and Junior? That might give you some peace of mind if either does."

"I've heard of that. I'll look into it, especially for the kitten." She gestured toward his nieces and her grandmother, who were taking turns holding Junior. "She's very attached to him."

Her mother reemerged from the house with a plate of foil-wrapped goodies.

Liam cupped his mouth and called out, "Time to go, girls."

"Oh, Uncle Liam, five more minutes," Madison said with a pout. "I haven't played with them enough like Katie."

"Your special time with the pets will be next Monday." He took the cookies from her mom's hands and held them up. "To tell you the truth, I didn't get enough chocolate tonight, so I may finish these chocolate-chip cookies if you don't come right away."

Katie walked toward him. "Can we have a couple before bed?"

"Yes." He turned toward Sarah and her mother. "Thanks for watching Katie and for these cookies." Then he started for the gate, peeling back the foil around the cookies.

Katie looked back at Madison but hurried toward her uncle. The gate closing caught Madison's attention. She hugged Gabe and Junior then ran to catch up with Liam and her sister.

"He's learning," her mother said.

"Yes, he's a good father to them in spite of what he thinks."

"He'll learn making mistakes is part of being a parent. Those two little girls have been a joy to have around. Even Nana has perked up with them here." Her mother sighed.

In a short time, Liam and the girls had ingrained themselves in her family. She really cared about Liam, but she was afraid there wouldn't be a good outcome for her and Liam—in spite of what her mother wanted.

Thursday evening Liam sat next to Colt at the high school pool while Katie and Madison practiced the new swimming stroke they were learning. "Beth was the first one into the water. Madison jumped right in, but Katie is my cautious girl." His youngest had been the last person in the pool, taking one slow step at a time into the water.

"Beth loves it. I just need her to do it better. I worry she'll sneak off and go swimming in the pond at the ranch."

"I'm glad the single dads' meeting is nearby. We'll be late as it is."

While Colt leaned forward, resting his elbows on his thighs, he watched his daughter swim across the pool. When she made it, he released a long breath. "That's the first time she's gone that far."

"Katie was so excited when she made it on Thursday. I was glad I was here to see it. That's all she talked about on the way home."

Colt slanted his head toward Liam. "That's the way Beth was when Madison asked her to her birthday party this Saturday. She had another hard day at school and that helped her forget about the kids making fun of her."

"Have you talked to the teacher?"

"Yes, but so far nothing has been successful. I'm looking forward to the summer. Hopefully next school year will be better. I'm going to talk to the principal and make sure my child gets the right teacher for her."

"Whereas I look at summer as another

change. We're just starting to get a routine down, and school will end and we'll have a new routine to get used to."

Colt chuckled. "Who's the routine for? You? Or your nieces?"

"Both. They do better with one and so do I."

"That's how I feel, too. Beth has to have one, but we'll fall into our usual summer one. The first summer will be the hardest as you find out what works and doesn't."

"What do you do with Beth when school is out?"

"I've tried a camp once, but it didn't go real well. A few years back I hired a person to look after her in the summer. They're at the ranch, and I drop in frequently to see how Beth is doing. Having someone gives me peace of mind about places like the pond or the field where the bulls graze."

As the class wound down Liam gathered his nieces' bags so they could change clothes in the dressing room. He stood off to the side as the girls exited the pool.

Katie and Madison hurried toward him.

"No running," Sarah called out and came toward him.

His nieces reached him at the same time with Madison saying, "Sorry. I forgot the rule."

"Me, too. We need to change and go with

Uncle Liam to a—" Katie looked up at him "—party."

Sarah smiled. "A party?"

Colt joined them with Beth.

"Yeah, with the dads' club. And I'm starving, so let's get ready." Madison tugged on her sister's arm.

"Can Beth go with you to the dressing room?"

"Sure." Madison took her bag and strolled with Beth to the door with Girl's Locker Room on it.

Katie walked—just short of running—to catch up with them.

"Beth is doing great. She wants to try everything," Sarah said to Colt.

"Thanks. Actually I owe Liam here big-time for telling me about these lessons. Sometimes I feel isolated at the ranch. Do you think they'll be all right by themselves in there?"

"Tell you what. I'll go see how they're doing."

Five minutes later the four of them walked out of the locker room.

Colt took Beth's hand and left the pool area while Liam paused next to Sarah. His nieces were becoming attached to her. What would happen when he wanted to leave Buffalo? There were times he thought about staying, but then he remembered the friends he'd left behind, his house, his connections…

"Liam, are you okay?"

He blinked at Sarah. "Sorry. Did you say something?"

"I just said you all better get going or the food will be gone."

"Yeah, we need to go."

The girls started for the exit.

He faced Sarah. "Thanks for everything. Madison has been talking nonstop about the birthday party."

"See you." Sarah headed for the pool.

Liam watched her and realized it wasn't only the girls who were becoming attached to Sarah. He was, too. As soon as the bachelor auction, swimming lessons and Madison's party were over, there wouldn't be a reason for them to see each other so much. That was probably for the best.

He rushed to catch up with his nieces, noticing Colt's truck was already gone.

A few minutes later he parked on the street several houses down from Michael Taylor's, right behind Colt. The girls ran to catch up with Beth and Colt, who'd stopped to wait for them.

"What did you bring?" Colt asked.

"A cake I baked earlier today. How about you?"

"The same. Store bought."

Michael greeted them when they entered the

house. "The kids are in the den. Carrie is in charge, much to her brothers' irritation."

"With a high-schooler at least you have a built-in babysitter," Liam said while Colt took his cake to the table then headed for the den.

"In between the debate team, soccer and school work. We were waiting for you two so we could start. Nathan has a problem concerning his ex-wife."

"Okay, let me put my—" Liam's cell phone rang, cutting him off. As he answered, another one in the living room went off, too.

"Liam here."

"We have a grass fire on the outskirts of Buffalo threatening a subdivision. Captain has called in all the firefighters," his lieutenant said.

"I'll be there as soon as I set up care for my nieces." While he disconnected, he saw that Brandon had also received a call.

His friend approached, frown lines slashing across his face. "I'll see you at the station."

Liam stepped out onto the porch to call Aunt Betty. The phone rang ten times before he finally hung up. He'd round up Madison and Katie and see if he could find his aunt.

When the three of them left Michael's house, Colt hurried after him. "Do you have someone to care for the girls?"

"Not yet. My aunt didn't answer her phone."

"Let me take your nieces, then."

"I'll probably be gone all night the way it sounds." Liam looked south and, in the dim light of dusk, could see the darkened sky that indicated a fire.

"That's okay. I'll make sure they get to school. Do you have time to get some clothes for them?"

"Yes. I'll bring back a bag."

"Good. Have Madison and Katie return here."

"Will do. Thanks." The scent of smoke laced the breeze from the south. He didn't have a good feeling about this. With the drought conditions the past few years, it wouldn't take much for a fire to get out of hand.

After he explained to the girls what was happening, he drove to his house to get them something to wear tomorrow. He set the bag on the patio and hastened to Aunt Betty's house. Lights were on in the kitchen. He knocked on the back door. Nothing. He went around to the front and rang the bell. Still nothing. He peeked into the garage window and saw that her car was gone. He'd try later. She didn't own a cell phone. He prayed he could get ahold of his aunt sometime tonight.

After dropping their bag off with Colt, he

kissed them each goodbye. He saw the worry in Madison's eyes and forced a smile to his face. "I'll be fine. I'm just going into work a little early."

"But what if…" She dropped her head.

"I've dealt with grass fires before, Madison. I'm counting on you being there for Katie if she gets upset. Okay?"

She nodded. "Okay."

He gave Madison a hug then Katie. As he drove away, he decided to swing by the pool to catch Sarah at the end of her last lesson. He had no reason to be worried about Aunt Betty, but he was. It was after dark, and she rarely drove anywhere at night.

As he pulled up, Sarah's car was still there. He jogged toward the building and pulled open the main door at the same time she pushed on it.

Surprise widened her gaze. "What's wrong?"

He quickly explained about the fire, Colt taking the girls for the night and Aunt Betty not being home. "I hate to ask, but will you try to get hold of her? I don't know when I'll be able to call her, and I would hate to wake her up."

"Sure. I'll take care of everything. I don't want you worrying about the girls or your aunt while working."

"Then I'll call you when I get a chance."

"I'll keep my cell phone by the bed, so even if it's after midnight, call me."

Her reassuring tone eased some of his anxiety. "You're a lifesaver."

"No, you are. Go do your job. I'm glad we live on the north side of town, but I'll be praying for the folks in the fire's path."

On impulse he clasped her arm and tugged her to him, kissing her—a brief connection he wished he could prolong.

He pulled away and ran to his car. As he backed out of the parking space, he couldn't shake the feeling that something was wrong.

Chapter Ten

Sarah paced the length of Betty's front porch, glancing at her watch every ten minutes or so. Finally at ten she glimpsed the woman's car coming down the street, probably at only ten miles an hour. The garage door went up as Sarah descended the steps and hurried to the driveway.

When Betty climbed slowly from her vehicle, the first thing Sarah noticed was the walking boot on her left leg. Then she saw Liam's aunt's face, an ashy cast to her features.

"What happened, Betty?"

"I went out to get the mail and fell off the curb. I drove myself to the emergency room. I didn't think I would be there so long, but there's a fire and a few people have been hurt."

"Liam has been worried about you. He's been trying to call you."

"I left him a message on his phone. He should have seen it by now since the girls need to be in bed because of school."

"You should have called Liam on his cell."

"I would have, but I don't remember the number. I usually call the house when I want to talk to him. I was at the hospital when I realized I'd left my address book at home." Betty limped toward the door into her kitchen, her jaw set as though she was in pain.

"Can I help?"

"Unless you can walk for me, no. The doctor gave me some pain meds to take once I got home." She unlocked her door and went inside. "Why has Liam tried to get hold of me?"

"He was called into work because of the grass fire."

"Where are Madison and Katie?" Grimacing, Betty clutched the counter to steady herself.

"Let me help you to your bedroom. Then you should take your meds and rest. The girls are with a friend, and I'll take care of them tomorrow afternoon and evening. You need to take care of yourself. And next time you can't get hold of Liam, call me. I can help. You shouldn't have driven yourself to the hospital."

"You were working."

"I could have figured something out. It's okay to ask for help."

Betty leaned against Sarah as she hobbled down the hall. "Then I'm asking. I need a few days before I look after the girls. My foot is throbbing and I have to go back in for it to be set and cast after the swelling goes down. Depending on what the doctor does, it may be hard for me to get around for a while."

"Don't worry. I'll work it out with Liam. Madison and Katie will be taken care of. You concentrate on getting better and, remember, when something like this happens, call us."

"I will. I realized it as I was driving to the hospital, but I was only a few blocks away so I kept going. I didn't have any way of getting hold of someone."

"Get a cell phone." Sarah helped Betty to her bed.

"I'm too old to learn something new." She sank down on her coverlet and handed Sarah her purse. "Would you please get me a glass of water? The meds I'm supposed to take are inside."

Sarah rummaged in the big purse, found two bottles of pills and put them on the nightstand. "I'll be right back with the water."

As she strode to the kitchen to get Betty's drink, she tried Liam's cell phone. After several rings, it went to voice mail. "This is Sarah. I'm at your aunt's house. She broke her foot and was at the hospital. She's home now and will be all right. Don't worry about the girls. Mom and I will take care of them tomorrow. Call when you get a chance. Stay safe."

As she filled a glass, something Betty had said resurfaced in her mind. People were being hurt enough to come to the emergency room because of the grass fire. And Liam was there to fight it. *Please, Lord, don't let one be Liam.*

When she took the water to Betty, she helped make her comfortable. "I'm going to stay for a while to make sure you'll be all right."

"They sent a walker home with me to help me keep my balance. It's still in the car. Will you please get it for me and put the garage door down?"

"Of course."

After retrieving the walker, Sarah stepped out of the garage. The smell of smoke overwhelmed her for a moment as she looked toward the south. Fire lit the dark night sky. Eerie. Menacing.

She shivered and couldn't get Liam out of her thoughts.

Please stay safe.

* * *

As dawn on Friday lightened the smoke-filled air, Liam trudged behind the anchor line, a gravel road, toward the refreshment table and snagged an ice-cold bottle of water and an energy bar. His legs felt as though he were carrying around twenty-pound concrete slabs. He collapsed on the ground near Brandon and removed his yellow helmet and black leather gloves.

After shoveling and raking for hours to make the fire lines, all Liam wanted to do was catch a catnap. But first a drink and food. "This fire isn't slowing down."

Brandon's tired eyes gazed at him for a long moment before he said, "If only the wind would die down, we might have a chance to contain this."

Liam bit off a piece of the energy bar. "We might not be able to protect those houses." He lifted his hand and pointed north toward Buffalo. "Especially if the wildfire jumps the highway and catches the woods between the subdivision and the road on fire."

"Yeah, and the wind is blowing in that direction." Brandon took out his cell phone. "I'm gonna check on my kids before we head back out."

Good idea. Liam retrieved his cell and noticed there was voice mail for him. He listened to the message from Sarah, his hand clutching the cell phone tighter as her words flooded his weary mind. He hated calling her when it was only a little after six, but he might not have another break for a long while.

He moved away from Brandon and placed the call. When she answered, the sound of her voice overwhelmed him with all the reasons he was falling in love with Sarah. Its warmth wrapped around him as though she embraced him.

"How's it going? Are you containing the fire?"

"It's still spreading. Pray for the wind to die down or a sudden downpour."

"I have been all night."

"Did you get any sleep?"

"Not much. How about you?"

"No. I have a break right now, but I might be too tired to sleep."

"You got my message?"

He closed his eyes, a vision of Sarah popping into his mind. "Yes. How's Aunt Betty?"

"I'm still at her house, and she's sleeping. She's worried about you. I told her you're too stubborn to have anything happen to you."

He chuckled.

"Liam, like I said in my message, don't worry about anything here. I'll take care of your nieces. When your aunt wakes up, I'll make sure she's all right before I leave. I'll pick Madison and Katie up from school. I'm going to stay with them at your house. That way I can check on Betty throughout the afternoon and evening."

"How about work?"

"I'm going to take the girls back to the salon and let them keep Nana company."

"Are you sure?" Liam took another swallow of the cold water.

"Nana said something about showing them Sammy. He's usually around the salon in the afternoon. She was excited and really looking forward to Saturday and Madison's birthday party. Don't worry about a cake. Mom has something in mind."

"What?" Liam imagined her sitting on his aunt's couch, her long, curly, blond hair framing her beautiful face.

"She wouldn't tell me. She's going to bake it tonight while I'm at your house. She thinks I might let it slip, and she wants Madison to be surprised."

An all-encompassing weariness enveloped him. "Thank you, Sarah."

"I can't fight the fire like you can, so I'm glad to do this to help."

"Talk to you when I can," he murmured, his eyelids sliding slowly down.

"Stay safe."

When he disconnected, he checked his watch. He had enough time to catch that nap his body was screaming he take. The last words Sarah said to him drifted through his mind as sleep descended.

Saturday morning Sarah found Madison outside in the backyard at Betty's house, staring south. A furrowed forehead and thin lips greeted her as the child glanced at her.

"Hon, are you okay?" Sarah purposefully stood in front of the girl, trying to block some of her view.

"It's twelve and Uncle Liam isn't here. It's so hazy I can't tell if the fire has been put out or not." Madison took a step to the right, her gaze glued to the sky.

Sarah put her arm around the child and peered south. "I was listening to the radio on the way from the salon and it looks like they're making some good progress toward containing the fire."

"He isn't gonna make my birthday party,

is he?" Madison blew out a sigh, her shoulders hunching.

"He'll be at your party if he can."

"It starts in two hours. He won't leave until the fire is out." Disappointment coupled with something Sarah couldn't pinpoint resonated in Madison's voice.

The light breeze carried the stench of smoke. "Let's go inside."

"What if he can't stop the fire? I have a friend who lives near it. She's supposed to come to my party."

Sarah hugged the girl against her. "If you're talking about Libby, her mom called the salon and let me know they would be there. They evacuated and are staying with relatives not far from here. Libby is really looking forward to your party."

"What if something happens to Uncle Liam? Have you heard from him since we talked with him last night?"

"No, but that doesn't mean anything."

She wasn't going to tell Madison because the firefighters were making a stand at the woods between the road and the subdivision, trying to put out any sparks that hopped the highway. The child was already worried enough—as was she. She'd refused to think what would happen if Liam was hurt. She'd prayed throughout the morning as she'd fixed her clients' hair and readied the salon for the party. Her mother had stayed a little longer to finish up.

"Nana came home with me. She was wondering where you were." Sarah held out her hand to Madison. "Let's go in. We still need to walk to my house and check on Gabe and Junior."

As Madison entered Betty's house first, Sarah's phone rang. "It's your uncle. I'll be inside in a minute."

Relief sagged Madison's shoulders even more.

Sarah took a few steps away from the doorway and waited until the little girl disappeared inside. "Hi, are you all right?" The question rushed out of her mouth before she could censor herself.

"Yes. It's been a long night. If nothing unforeseen happens, we should start the mop-up soon and make sure there are no hot spots that could start the fire all over again. How are the girls and my aunt doing?"

"Fine. They stayed with Aunt Betty for a couple of hours this morning. Betty seems to be better. At least her foot isn't hurting quite as much. She's keeping her foot raised and not walking on it a lot. Madison and Katie have been helping her."

"Good. Please let Madison know I'll make her party if at all possible. It'll depend on how fast the cleanup will be. Give both of them a hug for me."

"I will."

"Save the birthday cake until the end. Hopefully I'll be there by that time. I've got to go. The sooner we start, the sooner I'll be home."

Sarah's heart throbbed. The urge to put her arms around him and never let go swamped her. She wanted to make sure he was okay with her own two eyes.

The next ninety minutes went by fast. One of Betty's friends came to her place to keep her company. Madison and Katie kissed their great-aunt goodbye. Sarah promised Betty she would take a lot of pictures to show her.

Next stop was Liam's house, where the girls dressed for the party, then Sarah drove Nana, Madison and Katie to her house to make sure Gabe and Junior had food and water. At the salon fifteen minutes before the party was to begin, her mom met them at the door.

"I was about to send out a search team for you all."

Madison headed into the shop. "Junior got loose and was climbing the fence."

"I rescued him." Katie puffed out her chest. "I saw where he was before anyone else."

Madison stopped halfway through the salon and rotated slowly around, taking in the multicolored streamers from the ceiling, the big banner declaring she was eight years old today, the photo booth setup and the array of dresses and costumes. "You did all of this for me." The child faced Sarah and her mom, her eyes glistening. "It's perfect."

Emotions swelled into Sarah's throat. She swallowed several times. "Go into the back area and check out the decorated table—" she slid a glance at her mother who nodded "—with your cake on it."

A squeal pierced the air before Sarah entered the room. When she and her mom stepped inside, both girls were staring at the birthday cake.

Madison pointed at it. "It's like fingernail polish of my favorite color. Who made it?"

"My mom did. She loves to bake."

Madison swiveled around and rushed to Sarah's mother and threw her arms around her. "Thank you. It's the neatest cake I've ever seen. I love the pink."

Stunned, Sarah's mother was speechless as she peered down at the child and folded her in an embrace. When she glanced at Sarah, her eyes glistened. "I had so much fun making that, especially trying to figure out how to do the brush coming out of the bottle. It's strings of black licorice with pink frosting dripping off it."

"This is the best day ever!" Madison exclaimed, returning to stare at the cake.

Her expression solemn, Katie walked a few steps to Sarah's mom. "Will you make my birthday cake in October in the shape of a cat like Blackie?"

Her mother clasped her shoulder. "I'd love to, sweetie."

"Yay!" Katie pumped her arm in the air. "I agree. It's the best day ever!" Then she hugged Sarah's mom.

Her mother closed her eyes, but a tear slipped out and ran down her cheek. She turned away from Katie when the child pulled back. "Now I'd better get my supplies set up for the onslaught of girls in ten minutes."

Katie didn't see her wipe her hand across her face, but Sarah did. Her mom had wanted a house full of children, and in this moment Sarah wished she could give them to her. She would make a great grandmother.

She shuffled into the back room. "A car is parking. It's Britney. I've got everything set up to do everyone's nails."

"Good. We need an extra pair of hands." Sarah headed to the front to greet her friend. As she opened the door, Colt's truck pulled up with Beth smiling from ear to ear.

The next hour sped by with Sarah fixing hair while Britney helped the seven girls find the perfect costume and then ran the photo booth, which was a big hit. Occasionally, Sarah found herself checking out the window for Liam's car. If she could have postponed the party for a few hours, she would have, so he could have been there the whole time.

Katie, dressed in a purple ball gown with a tiara on top of her brown curls, motioned Sarah to lean down. The six-year-old whispered into her ear, "I'm starving. When are we gonna eat the cake?"

Sarah had been trying to delay the opening of presents and the eating of the goodies until Liam showed up, but she couldn't much longer. "Give me fifteen minutes. Beth is getting her nails done and they need to dry. Mom is almost finished with Libby's hair."

She dropped her head forward. "Okay."

Katie trudged away until Madison waved her into the photo booth for a picture with Ellie and her. She perked up and hurried toward her big sister.

As soon as Libby was done, Nana assisted

Britney to cram everyone into the booth for a group shot.

Sarah's mother joined her, watching the giggling girls juggle for a place. "The limousine is going to be here in forty-five minutes. We can't wait for Liam any longer."

"When they're through in there, we'll open presents then have cake and ice cream. I've taken some pictures of the cake for Liam."

"He's a good man."

"Mom, don't—"

"I'm not telling you anything you don't already know. He just spent nearly three days fighting a fire to protect this town. That's a hero in my book."

Her mother was right. Liam and the other firefighters often went above and beyond to do their jobs. She couldn't imagine how tired he would be. A flash of red out the front window caught her eye. On closer inspection, she grinned. "He's here. Just in the nick of time."

Her mother and Britney herded the girls to the back room while Sarah hung back and greeted Liam at the door. She wanted to wrap her arms around him and make sure he was all right. She didn't, but it was hard not to.

A grin dimpled his sun-kissed cheeks. "I would have been here sooner, but I didn't have

Madison's present. I had to swing by the house and retrieve it from my hiding place."

"They just went in for presents and cake. Perfect timing. You'll get to see the results of an afternoon at the beauty shop."

When Liam entered the back room, Madison spied him and cheered. As the other girls saw him, they did, too.

Libby approached him and embraced him. "You saved my house. Thank you."

His grin grew as all of the kids group hugged him. He stood in the middle of a crowd of girls, his face flushed as though the wildfire had scorched his cheeks.

Madison tugged him toward a chair next to hers. "I'm opening my presents now and just wait until you see what Sarah's mom made me."

While his niece tore into the first gift, Liam withdrew a small box from his pocket and put it with the others. He peered up at Sarah and winked.

Warmth flowed through her. He looked so capable and commanding in his navy pants and shirt with the fire department's emblem on it. The sight of him, exhausted but safe, caused her heartbeat to race.

He didn't give Madison his present until the end. When she ripped the paper off the box and lifted the lid, her mouth fell open. She held up the necklace for her friends to see. A gold heart-shaped locket dangled from the chain.

Her friends and Katie admired it while Madison leaned over and kissed Liam on the cheek. "I love it. Will you put it on me?"

Liam fumbled with the tiny clasp and finally tossed Sarah a look asking for help. She stepped in and, as he held his niece's hair up, she secured the necklace.

"It looks good with that dress. I hope you all are as hungry as I am." Liam tossed a glance toward the table with the treats.

"That's such a cute cake, are you sure you want to cut it?" Libby asked Madison.

Immediately all the other girls insisted on a slice. After they sang "Happy Birthday" to Madison, she cut the first piece, then Sarah's mother took over.

When everyone was served, Sarah and Liam sat in the two dryer chairs with a clear view of the back room.

She savored a couple of bites of the chocolate cake. "Mom outdid herself on this one."

"Mmm" was Liam's response as he shoveled another forkful into his mouth.

"You're hungry."

"I worked nonstop cleaning up rather than

taking a break, so I could get here in time. I didn't want to disappoint Madison."

"Both of them are having fun. Nana even promised them she would do their nails once a week. It'll be good for her."

"When I came in, your grandmother looked like she was having fun, too."

"How are *you* doing?" she asked casually, although she hadn't felt that way the past few days. She'd worried about him and hadn't been able to even listen to the news reports. She cared more for Liam than she realized. Thankfully his nieces and work had kept her attention most of the time.

"Tired. Glad the grass fire has been put out and grateful to you for your help. When I first came here, all I had was my aunt, but then I became involved with the single dads' group and I rescued a special dog." His golden-brown eyes gleamed. "With Aunt Betty's injury, it just shows me I need a backup plan if something happens."

"Another grass fire? I hope not."

"We need rain. I won't be surprised if we have more if it doesn't."

"How do you do it? Mom said something about the fire jumping the highway and consuming the woods between the subdivision and the road. All I could think about was a wall of flames coming at you."

He took her hand. "Fire can be unpredictable, but I've been trained well. Ultimately, I'm learning I have to put my life in the Lord's hands. I've seen Him do amazing things. Thankfully we managed to stop the fire before it took out the homes."

The rough texture of his touch attested to the job he had handling hoses and other fire equipment. "I've taken for granted firefighters and police officers. I don't think we realize how often you put your lives on the line for us."

He bent closer to her, his mouth hovering inches from hers.

Laughter drifted to her, and she pulled back, suddenly remembering seven little girls were nearby. "The limousine should be here soon."

Liam straightened and peered out the front window. "It's been out there for the past five minutes."

She rose and turned to look. "Why didn't you say something?"

"Because I was enjoying our talk."

"Where are the girls going?"

"The pavilion at the park." He shoved to his feet. "I'm so glad the air is starting to smell better. My backup plan would have been dinner at my house." He strolled into the back room and said to the group, "I've got another surprise for the birthday girl and her guests. Are you ready to go to dinner?"

Cheers greeted his question.

Ten minutes later the trunk of the limo was full of Madison's presents and any belongings the other girls had. Sarah's mom and Nana were going to clean the salon then meet them at the pavilion.

On the short drive to the park, Liam leaned his head against the back cushion. Slowly his eyes began to close in the midst of constant chatter from the girls. When the limousine stopped, he rallied himself and climbed from the car followed by Sarah.

She stared at the pavilion draped in pink cloth and balloons and white streamers. Brandon and Colt, dressed up in tuxedos, waited at the opening. As the girls piled out of the limousine, their eyes huge, silence reigned for a moment before they all started talking at the same time. Madison led the stampede toward the pavilion.

Liam clasped Sarah's hand. "Ready for hamburgers and fries served from my niece's favorite restaurant?"

"This is wonderful. And I can't believe Brandon is here."

"Me neither, but he'd told me he would do it

last week. As we left the grass fire, I told him to go home and get some sleep. He said no. He was looking forward to doing something uplifting." Liam started for the pavilion.

Sarah walked beside him, her heart melting at all the work he'd done for his niece. She knew it was time for her to deal with her grief, to move forward. She needed to say goodbye to Peter and to give her and Liam's relationship a chance.

His arms full of Madison's gifts, Liam entered his home, exhaustion he'd fought to hold at bay descending now that the birthday party was over. His nieces raced for the utility room to let the kittens out.

"Where do you want these?" Carrying some of the presents, Sarah stopped in the middle of the entry hall.

"In Madison's bedroom. Thanks for helping me bring them in. You should have let the limousine drop you off at your place. The girls could have helped me."

"I left Gabe here. At the time I wasn't sure you'd be able to make the party. He's out back."

"Okay. That must be why I hear the kitchen door slamming shut." At that moment the black Lab bounded down the hallway toward them.

Sarah greeted her dog then made her way up

the stairs to Madison's bedroom. Liam trailed behind her. This birthday party wouldn't have happened without Sarah. He was definitely falling for her. Would she be happy raising his two nieces? She would be a wonderful mother for the girls. Wow! Where were those thoughts coming from? He had plans for his future. Leaving Buffalo. Returning to Dallas, where he'd left behind thirty-five years of his life.

Deep in thought, he collided into Sarah in Madison's doorway. "Sorry. Wasn't paying attention." Everything was happening too fast. He felt as if he'd held his breath underwater longer than he should. His mind spun with conflicting emotions.

Glancing over her shoulder, she smiled. "That's okay. I have those moments, too." After placing the gifts on the bed, she returned to the hall with Liam and started for the staircase. "In your case, I'm surprised you're still standing upright. Why don't you go to bed, and I'll make sure the girls get to sleep at a reasonable hour?"

"I can't ask you to do that. You've put in a lot of overtime yourself. I can make it another hour or so. That is, if I can get the two to go to sleep." He sank on the couch in the den.

"Both of them have had quite a day. Tell

you what…I'll make you some coffee before I leave."

"Thanks. I'd do it myself, but this couch's arms are locked around me and holding me hostage."

Sarah chuckled and went to his kitchen. Soon she returned to the den, only to find him with his head against the back cushion, his eyes closed. She carefully set the mug on a coaster on the end table nearby then took the seat at the other end of the sofa. With a glance at her watch, she decided to stay and give the girls an hour before trying to round them up to bed and then she would go home.

Relaxing back, she thought about fixing a cup of coffee for herself but, like Liam, the comfort of the couch held her still. Slowly her eyelids slid closed and she gave in to the darkness…

Giggles and a cold nose nudging her hand pulled Sarah wide awake. She jolted up to find Madison, Katie and Gabe standing in front of her, the girls beaming.

"We wondered why no one told us to get ready for bed," Madison said while Katie held her hand over her mouth and snickered.

"Go get your pajamas on," Sarah whispered. "I'll come say good-night. We're letting your uncle sleep. He's had a long couple of days."

As soon as the girls left, she stood and snatched his untouched coffee—now cold—and drank half of it. If they hadn't woken her, she might have been there for hours.

After tucking each girl into bed, Sarah shut their doors and commanded Gabe to sit in the entry hall while she went to wake up Liam.

She hovered over him and shook his shoulders. "Liam, you need to get up. I'm going home."

Nothing.

She considered leaving him sleeping on the couch, but he didn't look very comfortable. When he did wake up, his muscles would ache. This time she raised her voice. "Liam. Liam," she said, trying to rouse him.

Finally his eyes blinked open then closed again. She scanned the den for a blanket or something to throw over him. When she peered back at him, he stared at her. Recognition dawned on him as he straightened, raking his hand through his hair.

"How long have I been sleeping?"

"Almost two hours. Madison and Katie have gone to bed. I'm leaving now."

He leaned forward, looking at the floor as though he was trying to figure out what she was saying. When he didn't say anything, she stepped back, turning to head to the front door.

He caught her hand and halted her escape. He pushed himself to his feet but swayed for a second.

Grabbing his upper arms, she steadied him. "Can you make it to your room?"

"Sure. I need to check the house to make sure it's locked up. I knew I was exhausted but not this much. I learned as a firefighter to wake up quickly. We never know when a call will come in. I'll walk you to the door and lock up after you go."

In the entry hall she turned to him to say good-night but no words came out. The intensity in his gaze captured her—as though he was really seeing her for the first time.

He cupped her face. "You're beautiful inside and out. Thank you for making this day so special for Madison."

"Both of your nieces are special to me."

He dipped his head toward hers, and his lips whispered across hers, sending goose bumps racing through her. His hands delved into her hair and pulled her against him. His arms locked around her as he deepened the kiss.

She became lost in his embrace, never wanting to end this bond that had been building for weeks.

When he finally stepped back, his gaze held hers as though his arms were still around her. Mesmerized by the golden sheen in his brown eyes, she struggled to picture Peter in her mind. She couldn't. Liam was all she saw.

Panic nibbled at her composure. Suddenly she fumbled for the doorknob behind her, managed to grasp it, then spun around and dragged the door open. "Good night," she murmured.

Halfway down the sidewalk, she slowed her pace, finally noticing Gabe was by her side. Liam made her forget everything. It was happening too fast.

Chapter Eleven

Monday morning Liam parked in Sarah's driveway and grabbed the container with the cookies the girls and he had made for Tina, Nana and Sarah. As he climbed from his car, he smiled at the memory of finding Madison and Katie trying to make the sugar cookies. It was reminiscent of the day Sarah had come to get Gabe, except he'd caught them before too much harm had been done.

This time, after his nieces had cleaned up the flour on the counter, they'd started over with his assistance. Once the baked cookies had cooled, Madison and Katie had spread frosting on each one and then halved them. That was when the real fun had started. Earlier he'd taken them to the store to find sprinkles and different kinds of decorative toppings for the cookies. The girls had spent an hour finishing the gift for the ladies who had thrown the best birthday party ever, as his nieces now referred to Saturday.

Liam mounted the steps to the porch and rang the bell. Sarah opened the door, ready to go with him to interview an auctioneer for the bachelor auction. But her gaze latched on to the plastic container he had.

"What's that?"

"A thank-you from the McGregory family for Saturday's party." He passed it to her.

"Why didn't they come later to deliver them?"

"Funny you should ask. Your mom has rubbed off on them. Last night when I went in to say good-night, Katie was in Madison's room, whispering. I heard enough to know they were going to have me bring them to you. Katie really needs to practice talking softly."

"But we'd already planned to see each other."

"They didn't know about us going to see the auctioneer for the fund-raiser. I tried to get them to give you the cookies after school today, but they insisted you needed them right away."

"I wonder if Mom has recruited them since I told her to stop." Sarah let him into the house.

"Maybe. When I dropped them off at school

this morning, Madison reminded me about the cookies. She's looking forward to seeing you today while I take Katie to dinner, so watch out."

"I'll put these in the kitchen and let Mom and Nana know about them. They're out back while Nana is trying to keep Junior from climbing the fence."

When Sarah left the room, Liam could still smell her fragrance with a hint of vanilla. Her scent brought another memory of last night to the foreground. Katie had poured too much vanilla into the cookie dough, causing him to try to spoon part of it out of the bowl.

"Ready?"

He turned toward her. Their kiss the other night crept into his thoughts. He wanted to blame it on being drowsy, but he couldn't. He'd known what he was doing and had enjoyed every second. "I'll feel better when we get an auctioneer."

"We have seventeen bachelors. We only need three more and possibly a couple of backup ones. In three weeks we've accomplished a lot."

He held the screen door open for her. "We work well together."

"I heard Beatrice is causing problems on the publicity committee. Oh, did I tell you that

Mom and I are forming a caregiver group that will meet next Sunday at the church?"

"Good. I look forward to the single dads' group meeting. I missed most of it last Thursday." Was there such a group in Dallas? Surely there was, and he could connect with it when he moved back. As the children grew older, he imagined different issues would surface, needing attention and advice on how to handle them.

As he drove to the county fairgrounds south of town, acres of burned vegetation lined both sides of the highway.

"I'm surprised the fairgrounds survived the grass fire. It was so near the area."

"But the wind blew in the other direction."

"Did anyone figure out how the fire started?"

"A dead branch fell on a power line and snapped it. It sparked what happened. When the conditions are as dry as they've been, it doesn't take much." Liam slid a glance toward Sarah after he parked at the main building at the fairgrounds. Maybe he wouldn't move to Dallas. He had a few months to decide.

A livestock auction was taking place inside. Liam and Sarah made their way toward the front as the last horse was bought.

"Mr. Caldwell is lively. He'll make it fun." Liam spotted the man leaving the stage and wove through the crowd to catch him. "Mr. Caldwell, may we have a word with you?"

"Sure. I'm finished for the day." The older gentleman wore wire-rimmed glasses and was completely bald.

"I'm Liam McGregory." He shook the man's hand. "And this is Sarah Blackburn. We're here to see if you would volunteer to be the auctioneer at the annual children's fund-raiser the first Saturday in June?"

"What would I be auctioning off? I assume that's what you want me for."

"Yes," Sarah said, "we're doing a bachelor auction at the end of the evening. We plan on having twenty men of various ages."

"Interesting. I usually handle items like cars, furniture and animals. Yes, I'll do it. It should be fun. I have a grandson the age of the children this fund-raiser will benefit. I'd love to do my part." He pulled a business card out of his shirt's top pocket. "Can you email me all the particulars? I'll put it on my calendar. I go to the fund-raiser every year."

Sarah took the card from him. "We have another favor to ask you. Will you agree to be interviewed as part of the publicity for the event?"

"As you probably saw, I love to talk, so why

not. Just let me know when and where and I'll be there."

After Liam and Sarah thanked him, they left. As Liam switched on the engine, he made a decision. He wanted Sarah and him to spend some alone time together. Usually his nieces and her family were with them. "It's lunch. I'd like to take you to the Sooner Boomer Café. Do you have time?"

"They have the best prairie salad."

"Prairie? Is it made with grass?"

"Cute. Not totally. There's green lettuce and spinach, feta cheese, glazed pecans, a fruit in season, tomatoes and strips of grilled buffalo meat."

"I've never had buffalo meat. Does it taste like chicken?"

She laughed. "No, it's like beef, and it's healthier and leaner than other meats. They have burgers made with buffalo."

"I'm game." Liam backed out of the parking space and drove toward the town. "I know that Colt raises buffalo on his ranch."

"Quite a few ranches in the area do."

As he headed for the café, he looked forward to getting to know Sarah more. There was something between them, and he wanted to explore it.

* * *

Sarah finished her last bite of the prairie salad and sat back as Liam signaled the waitress for a refill on his coffee. "Tell me something about you."

"I grew up in the Dallas area. Texas is in my blood."

"Then it must be strange being in the midst of us Okies."

He chuckled. "I've managed. Ever since I could, I've been a firefighter like my father. I like the challenges of the job."

"Are you a risk taker?"

He tilted his head to the side and stared off into space. When his gaze found hers again one corner of his mouth lifted. "I guess in some ways I am."

"What about now, with being the guardian of your nieces? Have you thought of doing something less risky?"

"I could worry about the future or just live it. I'm in God's hands and, as long as I'm doing something I love and helping others, I won't change."

"So you don't take precautions?"

"I didn't say that. When I was fighting the grass fire, I almost got caught with no way out. I didn't panic, but thought about my options, chose one and managed to get away from the flames. I've gone through extensive training."

Sarah's stomach plummeted. "Fire can be unpredictable."

"Life can be unpredictable. What good would it do to worry about the future when there's no way to predict what will happen? I tried to map my life out, and I thought I had it all figured out. Then something came out of the blue and changed everything."

"Your brother's death?"

"Yes, but before that, I was married. She walked out on me, leaving only a note."

"I'm sorry."

"We had problems like all marriages. I wanted to work through them. She didn't."

"Does she live in Dallas?"

"Yes, only a couple of blocks from me. She remarried as soon as she could."

Her heart ached for him. Before she'd dated Peter, she'd dated a guy who was in her classes at high school. When he broke up with her to date someone else, the worst part was seeing him every day until the end of the school year. "I know what you mean about having your life all figured out and suddenly everything changes. Peter died in a car wreck. I was driving. It wasn't my fault, but I used to run through the accident over and over in my mind, trying to figure out how I could have done something different."

Liam waited until the waitress refilled his coffee, then leaned toward her. "What happened?"

"An older man ran a stop sign and plowed right into the passenger side. Where Peter was sitting. We only had one car, and I needed it later so I took him to work. If only my appointment had been a different day. If only I had swerved and avoided the wreck. If only…" Her throat closed around the scenarios she used to run through that would have left her life on the same course. Or would it? Liam was right. They didn't know what was going to happen in the next ten minutes, let alone the next ten years.

Liam touched her hand resting on the table between them. "Were you injured?"

She fiddled with her spoon by her plate, toying with telling Liam everything. She was tired of avoiding the subject. That hadn't done any good. Avoidance didn't mean it would go away. "Most of my injuries healed quickly. Except one. I was five months pregnant and lost my little girl."

He tightened his hand over hers. "I'm so sorry. That doesn't even begin to tell you how I feel."

"For months I dreamed of the day my baby would come into this world. I didn't consider she would die. I've always felt I would be a mother. Still feel that way. Have you ever known something deep down?"

For a long moment he stared at the table between them. When he raised his gaze, a shadow darkened his eyes. "I knew I would follow in my father's footsteps. I wanted to continue my dad's heritage. I wanted to belong to his fire station. Those guys all became like a father to me. My captain in Dallas was my dad's best friend. I miss talking to him."

"Have you talked to him much since you moved here?"

"About once a week. It's nice hearing about what's going on, but mostly just talking with someone back home."

"When I lived in Tulsa, I missed Buffalo and talked to my mom often."

"Why did you leave?"

"When Peter died, I didn't want to leave Mom's house. I couldn't live in mine anymore, but I also had a hard time dealing with going other places. I couldn't move to another part of town like a person could in Dallas and create new memories. I had to move away. I needed to start over."

"Now you're back here. What's different?"

"You ask tough questions." She sucked in a deep breath, held it for a few seconds then slowly exhaled. She wished she could deal with pain that easily. The compassion in his eyes urged her to trust him and let another one in again. "Time, partially. My mom needed me to help with Nana, and I'm finally realizing I can't move on without letting go of the past once and for all. Not forget it, but release its hold on me."

"Have you?"

"I'm getting there. I can drive by the intersection where the wreck occurred without falling apart. That's actually where I found your poster about Gabe."

"So we might not have met if you hadn't."

"I like to feel Gabe would have found his way home, but he loves your nieces."

"Having him there even for a few days showed me that a pet would be good for the girls. They take care of their kittens. They make sure they have water and food. They clean their litter box. But, mostly, they have bonded with Buffy and Blackie. So a lot has changed since I met you, and it's been good."

"I notice Madison talks to you more and doesn't get as angry at Katie."

"I've gone to say good-night to her and often find her talking to Buffy. She's been telling

Buffy about her dad. I still wish she would come more to me about Gareth."

"Each person has to find their way through their grief. Maybe Buffy is Madison's." *You're becoming mine.* That thought stunned her and, for a few seconds, the world seemed to come to a stop. No, that wasn't possible. She'd only known him a month.

"But I want my nieces to know they can come to me. I may not be their father, but I love them like a dad."

"A person might not be someone's birth father, but that doesn't mean he doesn't play the role of one."

The waitress placed the bill on the table. "Do y'all want anything else? Dessert? We have a great peach cobbler."

"I still have a few errands to do before I watch Madison." She'd been putting off going to Peter's and Emma's graves for a while. It was finally time.

"Same here." He withdrew his wallet and put some cash to cover the tab on top of the receipt. "Keep the change."

"Thanks. Have a great day." The waitress removed some of the dishes and left.

Sarah rose at the same time as Liam. As they walked to his SUV, he was silent. The quiet continued on the way to her house.

When he pulled into her driveway, he stared out the windshield as though in deep thought.

Finally he looked at her and smiled. "I enjoyed lunch." He cradled her face between his rough palms. "You've helped me finally figure out what I need to do."

She returned his grin. "Talking to you has been good for me, too." She took one of his hands and kissed his palm. "Now I'd better get going, or I won't be here for Madison."

She scrambled from the car before she lost her nerve to go to the cemetery. She'd shared a part of herself she didn't with others, and it felt right. A lightness to her step, she went inside to let her mother know her plans. She found Nana and Mom out back chasing Junior around the yard. With Gabe next to her, she watched and tried not to laugh out loud.

"Gabe, fetch Junior."

Her black Lab raced down the deck and across the yard. He cornered the kitten and gently took him into his mouth and trotted to Nana. Sarah's mother plodded to her, out of breath.

"I'm exhausted. Junior climbed the fence again. Then we finally got him down, and he scurried past us and up the fence on the other side. I think I've got my quota of exercise for the week."

"Mom, it's time to let Junior leave the yard if he does. He has his tracker on, and we can find him if he gets lost. He's at least three months old."

"But what if something happens to him?"

Sarah thought about staying up late worrying about whether Liam would get hurt or not fighting the grass fire until finally she'd given his safety to God. "Trust the Lord. I know what it's like to hold on to something too much."

"I know, but Nana doesn't."

"She does, if you will. I came out here to tell you that I'm going to the cemetery, but I'll be back for Madison."

"Oh, sweetie, I'm so glad you're going. Don't worry about Madison. I was going to show her how to French braid her hair today. She's been asking about it. Stay as long as you need."

"Thanks, Mom."

Twenty minutes later Sarah stood in front of Peter's headstone for the first time since she'd left Buffalo. She knelt between his and Emma's graves and pulled several weeds that had encroached on their plots.

"Peter, we had a great marriage. For a while I didn't think I could ever find someone like you, but I have—at least I think so. I'm falling in love with Liam. He has the same caring and compassion you had." She switched her attention to Emma's small grave. "Darling, I wish I could have been your mother, but God had different plans. I know you're in good hands. I love you and that will never change."

Finally she rose and dusted off her jeans. She blew a kiss to each one then swung around and made her way to her car. She could move on now and hopefully one day have her own family.

Later that evening Liam and Katie strolled toward Sarah's side gate. She'd said they would be in the backyard if it was still light.

"He's been gone for twenty minutes, Sarah. He's lost." The sound of Nana's raised voice drifted to him and Katie.

Katie peered up at him. "Junior is gone! We've got to find him."

Liam opened the gate. "Let's check to see what happened. If we need to help, we will."

Katie ran ahead of him to Nana while Liam detoured to Sarah and Madison working on homework on the deck.

"What's going on? Do we need to search for Junior?" Liam stood across from Sarah. Looking at her, he realized if he pursued his feelings for her he would end up hurt. After what she'd told him at lunch, she could never be satisfied with being a mother to Katie and Madison. She wanted children he couldn't give her.

"Every five minutes, Nana has been announcing how long Junior has been gone. He finally climbed over the fence," Sarah said.

"And you're not concerned?"

Madison put her pencil down and closed her notebook. "Junior has a tracking collar on." She gestured toward the cell phone on the table by Sarah's arm. "He's next door."

"They don't have any animals, and he's checking out his surroundings." Sarah rose. "I've told Nana that, but I'm going to show her this. If that isn't enough to convince her, I'll take her right to Junior."

Liam glanced at her grandmother. Katie had helped her to her feet then walked with Nana toward the deck. Sarah met her at the bottom of the steps.

"Sarah, it's been twenty-five minutes. I haven't forgotten how to tell time."

"Nana, I told you I know where Junior is. He's nearby."

"How? Do you suddenly have X-ray vision?" Her grandmother pinched her mouth in a firm, thin line.

"No, I have this." Sarah held up her phone that showed the kitten's tracking.

Nana folded her arms over her chest. "That's a blinking dot. That's not Junior."

"I'll show you. We're going to follow this blinking dot to his location about thirty feet to the right."

Nana marched toward the gate. "C'mon, Sarah. It's getting dark."

Liam dipped his head toward Sarah and whispered, "We'll leave you to deal with your grandmother. If you need us to help find Junior, just give me a call. Thanks for watching Madison."

"Anytime." Sarah hurried to Nana.

"Ready, you two? Katie, do you have any homework?"

His youngest shook her head.

"And I'm finished with mine. So, Katie, we'll have time to play with our kittens. I'll race you home."

"Hold on. No running until we cross the street. Then, if you want to, you can." Liam followed them, making sure the gate was closed.

"Can we race to the corner and wait for you?"

"Yes."

The second he said that his two nieces charged down the street. Liam looked toward the neighbor on the right as Sarah and her grandmother emerged from their backyard.

Nana grinned from ear to ear while cradling Junior against her.

As he headed down the street, he knew he needed to put some distance between him and Sarah. He didn't just care about her. He was falling in love. He'd already been devastated from one woman leaving him because he couldn't father children. He wasn't sure he could handle that from Sarah.

But even after tucking the girls into bed, he couldn't rid his mind of Sarah. She haunted his thoughts as if she'd already claimed his heart. What was he going to do?

At the fund-raiser meeting, Liam sat at the other end of the table from Sarah. He'd purposefully come late to avoid being near her during the luncheon and updates from each group, but when they broke up into subcommittees, he was stuck being closer. A couple of times he'd caught her looking at him with a puzzled expression. He hadn't seen her in a week except briefly at church, where he'd herded his nieces out of the building before she could come over to speak to them. He knew he couldn't keep doing that. He had to talk to her. Especially since the girls kept asking where she was.

"Okay, it's settled, then. After the posters are printed up next week, we'll each take a section of town and be responsible for putting them up, especially in any business that will let us." Pastor Collins closed his notebook.

"Thanks to everyone." Sarah's gaze skimmed the faces of each member of the bachelor auction committee, resting a few heartbeats longer on Liam than the others. "Other than last-minutes details, we are all set for our part of the fund-raiser."

"I forgot to mention that I arranged for the weekend newspaper to interview our bachelors and run a feature on the auction the week before the fund-raiser. Do you and Liam want to call the men you recruited, or do you want me to do it?" Beatrice divided her intense focus between him and Sarah.

He started to tell her she could when Sarah chimed in, "We will. Just give us all the details."

Sarah said *we* and *us*—as if they were a couple. Liam shifted in his chair, feeling the need to escape.

"Suit yourself," Beatrice murmured and gathered her purse from the floor then stood.

Brandon's subcommittee was still meeting across the room. Liam needed to talk to him and would have to wait outside until they were through.

But before he could move, Sarah took the

chair next to him. "I realized I jumped in and answered Beatrice without consulting you. If you can't make the calls, I'll do them all."

"No, I'm fine with it. Let me know when you get the information from her. I'm not particularly looking forward to being interviewed."

"Why? It should be fun."

"Not for someone who doesn't like being in the limelight."

"Then why did you say yes to being one of the bachelors?"

"Because some of the guys wouldn't do it unless I did. Besides, it's for a good cause. I've already signed my girls up for camp this summer. They're so excited. They loved it last year."

"How's everything? Gabe has missed the girls. I imagine Buffy and Blackie are demanding their full attention when they come home from school."

"Those two are active kittens, always getting into trouble. Buffy found a grocery store plastic bag on the floor in Madison's room and ended up trapped with it around her. She went flying up and down the hall trying to shake it. We finally found her downstairs hiding behind the couch, shaking like a leaf in a windstorm. I moved it so Madison could rescue her. It took an hour to calm her."

Sarah laughed. "It sounds like a cat. They are curious creatures."

"How's Nana's kitten getting along? Any problems with your mother's allergies?" The questions came out before he could stop himself. It was so easy to talk to Sarah. He would miss her conversation and company, but he needed to keep his distance or, before he realized it, he would be totally in love with her. The problem was that for the next month they would have to work together, and he couldn't avoid that. And then there were his nieces, who were always talking about Sarah.

"Nana is great. Her life revolves around Junior now. And, surprisingly, she hardly messes up with anything dealing with Junior. She often takes my cell phone outside in case he leaves the yard."

"I know the kittens have helped my nieces. I'm glad it's working for Nana, too." Out of the corner of his eye, he noticed the last subcommittee was through. He stood. "Sorry, but I need to catch Brandon."

"And I need to get back to work. Bring the girls by when we're home. Nana and Mom love seeing them."

"I will." He crossed the room to snag Brandon before he left. Maybe he could time his visit when Sarah was gone. But then every time he thought of not seeing her, bleakness settled into his thoughts. "Brandon, do you have a sec to talk?"

His friend stopped and grinned. "For you, yes. I wasn't sure you were going to come."

"Yeah, I was running late." Liam panned the room. Empty. "I need some advice, and our single dads' next meeting isn't until a week from Thursday."

"Sure. This sounds serious."

"You've talked about some of your difficulties with your two sons when you decided to move back here after your wife died. Why did you come back?"

"I grew up here, and this town is a great place to raise children. Besides, I had friends and some family living in Buffalo."

"How did you handle the move with your boys?"

"Are you thinking of leaving for Dallas?"

"Yes. All along I had intended to stay here a year then return to Dallas, but now I'm thinking of doing it in August before the girls start school. I figure a move in the middle of a school year could be harder."

Brandon whistled. "I didn't even know you were considering it. The guys will miss you—" he cocked a grin "—mostly because of your cooking, but your firefighting skills ain't bad, either."

"Nothing like a shower of accolades to get a guy to stay."

"I aim to please." Brandon's smile faded and a thoughtful expression fell over his features. "Seriously, it was not a fun time for us. The kids came here kicking and screaming. Seth was eight and he was the worst. I think Jared only acted out because his older brother did."

"They seem well adjusted to Buffalo now. How long did it take?"

"Not long at all for Jared. However, Seth was a whole different story." He tilted his head. "But now that I think about it, Seth was having a hard time in Saint Louis. He took his mother's death harder than Jared."

"Like Madison."

"It's been over six months. Is she still giving you problems?"

"Not as much, especially since she got Buffy for a pet."

"Seth still says he wants to go back home, but usually when he's mad at me. Otherwise, he's happy here."

"So how did you handle Seth when he acted out?"

"Just like I would before. I understood where he was coming from, but I couldn't let him get away with that kind of behavior. No one likes change, but it happens. I didn't move here to teach them that, but it has. I'm the same. Our furniture and possessions are the same."

"Any suggestions?"

"Once you know for sure you're gonna leave, start preparing them. Give them time to adjust to what's coming. That's always a good thing to do. And, yes, I think it would be better if they start the school year at the beginning. Schools change the make up of a class every year, so there will be plenty of kids who don't know anyone in their class."

"I hadn't thought about that. They won't feel they're the only new kid. Thanks, Brandon. This past weekend I spent Saturday going through the house to see what I needed to paint or fix. There's a lot to do."

"If you need any help, let me know. I could bring the boys over and they could play in the backyard with your nieces." Brandon walked toward the exit.

"I may have to take you up on the offer. If I move in August, I'm going to be busy for the next few months." That would be a good thing. It would keep him from thinking about Sarah and wanting to spend time with her.

"That means you need to tell the girls about

your plans. They might be angry, but it'll give them time to adjust to the idea of moving."

"When?" Liam voiced the question he'd been thinking.

"Soon. They'll know something is up if you're fixing up the house." Brandon added, "Get some suggestions from the other guys at our single dads' meeting next week."

"Thanks, I will. That's one of the things I'll miss. I haven't been a member long, but it's been good knowing I'm not alone."

"There should be something like our group in Dallas. If not, start one. I hear Tina is starting a caregiver support group at the church." Brandon stepped outside, dark clouds roiling across the sky. "Looks like we might get rain finally."

On the drive home sprinkles spattered Liam's windshield. As he pulled into the garage a downpour fell from the sky. With the door still up, he stared at the rain drenching the earth and running in rivulets to the street.

Maybe this weekend or next he would talk to Madison and Katie. But should he do it with them together or separated? He wanted to ask Sarah's opinion. He couldn't. He needed to sever those ties as much as possible.

On Thursday of the following week Liam climbed from the car, rounded to the trunk and removed a folding chair and a cooler with a cherry-flavored Jell-O mold with pecans, carrots and pineapple inside. He wasn't a big fan of it, but the girls loved it.

Madison and Katie ran toward the other kids playing near the pavilion at the park that was set up for the single dads' barbecue. As he headed for the area the men had staked out to sit and watch their children play an impromptu soccer game, he'd recalled how he almost had to drag his nieces from their swimming lesson—and Sarah. Even from where he'd sat in the stands, he'd heard both of his girls complaining they wanted to see Sarah more often. Then they'd begun whispering between themselves and then to her. They were up to no good, but he hadn't had time to talk with Sarah to see what they were plotting.

Liam set up his folding chair next to Brandon's and sank onto it, tired from spending the day painting the living room a neutral color.

His friend leaned toward him. "You haven't told Madison and Katie yet, have you?"

"Why do you say that?"

"Because they seem downright happy."

"And if I tell them, they won't be?"

Brandon arched an eyebrow. "You forget, I've been through it."

For some reason Liam couldn't bring himself to tell his nieces about moving in the middle of August. It would make it so final, and their recent calm home would be disrupted.

"Liam, are you sure moving is the best answer?"

"Yes." No, he truly wasn't. Seeing Sarah today at the swimming pool had been the highlight of his day.

Brandon signaled everyone to move in closer. The circle of chairs shrank. "Liam needs some help." In a low voice his friend told the group about his decision to leave Buffalo in August. "When and how should he break the news to his nieces?"

"Wait until you have to put up the for-sale sign," Nathan said before another dad punched him in the arm.

Michael checked the kids before saying, "Knucklehead, that would lead to more problems. You've got girls. You should do it now and then prepare yourself for dramaville."

By the end of the brief conversation Liam's head pounded with tension. The consensus was that he should tell the girls this Sunday after church. He couldn't put it off any longer. And if he was going to tell them, he needed to let Sarah know first. He didn't want her to hear it from Madison or Katie.

He searched the makeshift soccer field and

found Madison with the ball dribbling past Katie and Jared before Seth stole it from her and went in the opposite direction. He'd played soccer as a child. He wondered if one of the girls would.

When he shifted his attention, it landed on Sarah with Gabe standing under an elm tree watching the soccer scrimmage. Now he knew what his nieces had been up to at the pool.

He rose, glancing down at Brandon. "Will you keep an eye on Madison and Katie? If I'm going to tell them about the move, I need to let Sarah know, too."

"Now?"

His posture straightened with determination. "Yes." *Before I lose my nerve.*

Madison spied Sarah, waved and started toward her. When she saw Liam approaching, his niece halted and returned to her buddies.

Sarah smiled as he joined her and Gabe. "The girls begged me to bring Gabe to the park while they were here. It's hard to say no to them."

"Believe me, I know. Can we go for a walk?"

Her forehead scrunched. "Sure. Is something wrong?"

It continually amazed him how in tune Sarah was with him. "I wanted to talk to you about something before I tell the girls."

"This sounds serious." She set off on the trail away from the pavilion.

Halfway between the group and the street, Liam gestured toward a bench off the walking path. "Let's sit. It's been a long day, but I finished painting the living room."

"Didn't you tell me on Tuesday you did the den?"

"Yes." He eased onto the wooden seat and sighed as his body continued to wind down.

While Gabe sat and looked toward the children, Sarah said, "What's been going on lately? Something is different since Madison's birthday party."

"I think I mentioned to you when I first came here that my plans were to return to Dallas in a year after my nieces had a chance to get used to me. After much consideration, we're leaving before school starts. I haven't told them yet, but I think that would be a better time to make the transition."

Her gaze dropped away from his. Her hands squeezed into tight fists, her knuckles turning white. "I see." She bolted to her feet and said, "Tell Madison and Katie I needed to get home," then she called Gabe and bolted off down the street.

Chapter Twelve

"I'm not going to cry. I'm not!" Sarah muttered to herself as she put as much distance as possible between her and Liam.

But in spite of her resolve, tears leaked from her eyes and rolled down her cheeks. She wiped them away in angry strokes. She'd begun to visualize herself with Liam as more than a friend. She'd been a fool to fall for him. He had said something to her about possibly leaving Buffalo. Why did she think he would change his mind? That she would be a good reason to stay here?

"Sarah, wait up."

She glanced back, saw Liam and increased her pace. She couldn't see him while she was crying. She glimpsed the street where she lived. More importantly, she didn't want her mother to see them. Coming to a halt, she fought to control her emotions before she faced him.

She wanted to scream, "Why are you leaving now? When I want you to be part of my life? When I love you and your girls?" The last question slammed into her with such force she closed her eyes and stepped back, desperately wanting to be anywhere but there. She was in love with him, and he was leaving.

He clasped her arms. "Sarah, are you all right?"

Needing to retain some of her dignity, she inhaled a breath and opened her eyes. "Yes. What else do you have to say? I think your leaving says it all. This was just a temporary stop for you. I don't blame you. You've always said you miss Dallas."

"I lived there thirty-five years. Put down roots there."

"You can put down roots anywhere. What's wrong with Buffalo?"

"Nothing. It's a beautiful town, and I've enjoyed getting to know people." He released his grasp and looked away.

"But?"

"Being a single dad is hard. I need my support system. I never intended to stay here when I came."

"You have a great support system here."

She waved her hand toward the park. "What about the men you've gotten to know in the single dads' group or the firefighters you work with? What about me and my family, and even Betty? Do we not count?"

He clamped his jaws together so tightly a muscle twitched. "It's complicated."

"I'm not going anywhere. Explain why it's complicated, so I understand. I thought we had something between us. I…I care about you."

"I know we're friends, and I appreciate that, but…" His voice trailed into silence.

"To me it's much more than friends. I'm falling in love with you, Liam."

He frowned.

Anger surged in her. "That's okay. It's my problem. Not yours." She swung around to leave.

He grabbed her. "Wait. I'm falling in love with you, too, Sarah."

Confusion mingled with the fury. "Then why are you leaving?"

Raking his hands through his hair, he turned in a slow circle as though making sure no one else was around. When he faced her again, his eyes held sorrow. "Because I can't give you the one thing you want. Children. My ex-wife left me because I couldn't give her a child. We tried for several years then went for testing to see if there was a problem. I was the problem. I have a genetic disorder that affects my fertility."

His news sent a shock wave through her. Her mind blanked.

"So you see, there could be no future for us, and I can't stay here and see you without wanting you."

All she could think to say was, "I'm sorry, Liam. I—"

"Don't say anything else. Nothing will change it. You're the only one who knows besides my ex-wife and, believe me, she let me know how she felt about it. Although I've had the genetic defect all my life, I didn't know until we went for testing. My case was mild, so other symptoms didn't cause concern. It isn't something I tell others when I meet them, so please don't tell anyone."

"I would never do that."

A neutral expression dropped over his face. "Thank you for that. Now, I need to get back to the park."

She took a step toward him as he hurried away. What could she say to make him feel better? His ex-wife must have really done a number on him. When he disappeared from view, she walked in the direction of her home, completely numb.

A few minutes later she stood in front of her house but couldn't bring herself to go inside. Her mother knew she had gone to the park to see Liam and his nieces. She would have questions she didn't want to nor could answer. Putting one foot in front of the other, she continued walking down the street.

After the park and his encounter with Sarah, Liam had to tell Madison and Katie they would be moving. If he could leave right now, he would. Telling Sarah had been the hardest thing he'd ever done. He wouldn't forget her face when he'd told her he couldn't have children. Shock and even anger had flitted across her features. She hadn't said the hurtful, demeaning words that Terri had, but she had to be thinking them.

Terri's reaction had taken him through the grieving stages. He was starting to accept his circumstances and moving on with his life, but the anger stage had left its mark on him.

He climbed the stairs to talk with Katie first. He'd decided to do each one separately. He hoped that Katie would be more agreeable, while he *knew* Madison wouldn't be. He didn't want her first reaction to color Katie's. In time, he prayed they both would accept the decision and learn to love Dallas as he did.

When he entered her bedroom, Katie put a toy back on the shelf and scurried to her bed. She pulled the covers over her legs and sat with her back against the headboard while Blackie snuggled against her.

A smile brightened her features. "I had a great time tonight. I want to play soccer in the fall."

He sat on the edge of the bed and twisted toward her. "I played soccer in Dallas as a boy. They have a good league in the area where I live. I even helped coach a team last year."

"Are you good?"

He chuckled. "The team won their division."

"Wow. Will you help me learn the game?"

"I sure can." He hated to turn this conversation into a serious one, but he had to. "Listen, Katie, I have something important to tell you."

She caught sight of something on her desk and covered her mouth with her fingers. "I forgot. I meant to take that bowl downstairs before I went to bed. I can right now."

He placed his hand on her arm. "Stay. I'll take care of it this one time." He searched his mind for a good way to start. "You would like Dallas. I live north of the city. There is so much to do around where I live. Some of my firefighter buddies have boats on a nearby lake, and we spend a lot of time there."

"Are there kids at the lake?"

"Sure." He looked into her blue eyes. "When I came to Buffalo, I'd planned to stay here about a year then move back to Dallas with you and Madison."

"You did? Why?"

"Because Dallas has always been my home. You even have some cousins that live near me."

Her eyes grew round.

"I was going to wait until November 1 to leave when the lease on my house was up, but I contacted the renter and he'll leave earlier if I want. I think it would be better for us to move to Dallas before school starts in mid-August."

Her forehead crinkled. "We're moving?"

"Yes, by August 15."

She frowned. "Why can't we stay here?"

He couldn't tell her the main reason concerning Sarah, but he would give her what he'd felt when he first came. "I think it would be good to start new as a family. I love you and Madison, and I want us to create our own memories at the lake or playing soccer."

"I can play soccer in Dallas?"

"Absolutely. I would love to have someone to cheer for."

She pointed to herself. "Me?"

"Yes. Like my mom used to cheer for me."

"Uncle Liam...can I call you Daddy?"

Tears welled up in his eyes. After the news from the doctor about his genetic disorder, he'd never thought he would ever be called Daddy or Dad. "I'd be honored if you did, Katie."

"Will I have my own bedroom in Dallas?" He nodded.

"Can I take Blackie?"

"Most definitely."

She picked up her kitten curled up on the pillow next to hers. "Did you hear that, Blackie? You and me are going to Dallas with Daddy!"

"Daddy's dead and I won't go to Dallas," Madison screamed from the doorway then ran to her room. She slammed the door closed so hard a picture on the wall fell to the floor.

When Liam glanced at Katie, she held Blackie up against her cheek. "She's mean. It always has to be her way."

"She's upset. I haven't told her yet."

Katie lifted her chin. "Then she was spying on us, and that's wrong."

"I need to talk to her. I don't know how much she heard, but I want her to know everything we talked about. Are you okay with that?" He rose.

Katie nodded.

Liam kissed her cheek. "I love you, Katie."

As he strode toward the hallway, his niece said, "I love you, Daddy."

At the door Liam turned toward Katie. His heart swelled in his chest, making taking deep breaths hard. He flipped off the overhead light while she squirmed beneath the covers. "Good night." He closed her door so Blackie would stay put.

Liam continued to Madison's bedroom and knocked. When she didn't say anything, he turned the knob. The door was locked. "Madison, we need to talk. Open the door."

"Go away. I don't want to."

"We still need to talk."

"No," she sobbed.

Liam descended the stairs and made his way to the den at the back of the house. In the desk he had a device to unlock any door. This would be the first time he used it. He clutched it and began pacing. Maybe he shouldn't. He could try later when she was calmer. Or, if he had to, he could tomorrow. He didn't go to work until Saturday. If she was angry, she wouldn't listen to him.

What do I do, Lord?

The only words that came to mind were to be patient.

Liam switched on the TV to break the silence of the house and take his mind off what had happened with Madison. No matter how much he'd prepared himself for her fury, it still left him doubting himself.

An hour later he climbed the stairs to check on Madison to see if she was ready to talk to him. He rapped on the door several times and even asked her to open up. Nothing. He tried the knob, and it turned. When he went into her room, it was empty except for Buffy sleeping on the bed.

He looked in her closet and even under the bed then went in search of Madison. She wasn't in Katie's room. In fact, his youngest niece was sound asleep and didn't even move when he came in to check for her older sister.

His bedroom and a spare one were empty, as well. He'd combed the bottom floor half-way when he received a call on the landline. He snatched up the receiver. "Liam here."

"Madison came to see me. I wanted you to know so you wouldn't get upset if you couldn't find her."

He leaned against the counter in the kitchen. He really wasn't that surprised Madison had snuck out to see Sarah. "I hate to ask, but could you bring her home? Katie is already asleep."

"May I talk to her for a little while first? That's why she came, and I think she needs someone to listen to her."

"I wanted to. She didn't want to."

"I figured that. Someone…besides you."

"Fine. If you can help her, I'd appreciate it." When he hung up, he sank into a chair at the kitchen table.

Lord, what do I do?

"He never listens to me. He does what he wants. Forget about Katie and me." Madison sat on Sarah's deck. Even in the dim shadows of the single light, Sarah saw the battle of Madison's emotions in her eyes. They were swollen, and tears ran down her face as she worked herself up about the move to Dallas. Through the sadness emerged anger—even fear—from her scowl to her nervous habit of chewing on her bottom lip.

When Madison first showed up, Sarah had a hard time coming up with words of comfort when inside she hurt for the exact same reason, except that Madison would go with Liam. He would leave Sarah behind. She'd barely had time to process what he'd told her earlier about not being able to have children before the girl appeared.

"Your uncle loves you very much and is very concerned about you two. That's why he's moving to Dallas before school starts rather than move you in the middle of a school year."

"I don't want to go. Why can't he stay and work here?"

Because of me flashed into Sarah's mind. Now that she knew he couldn't have children, did she want him to stay and see him all the time? "Until he came to Buffalo, Dallas was the only home he knew. He has friends and relatives there. Those relatives are yours, too."

"He has friends here. Aunt Betty is here. She's family. Please talk to him. Change his mind."

"It's not my decision. I know he didn't make this decision lightly. You need to tell him what you're telling me. You told me you wouldn't talk to him. But you owe him that much. He left everything to come to Buffalo and take care of you and Katie."

"And now he wants us to leave everything."

"He loves you. Family is important to him. Promise me you'll talk to him. Give him a chance. Will you?"

Madison stared at her lap.

Sarah waited for her to reply. This wouldn't be easy for Madison, but then, it wasn't for Liam, either. She was the reason he was leaving Buffalo. She didn't want him to, but she understood why he was. She'd fled town after her husband died. The town was small enough that anywhere she went she was constantly reminded of Peter. Could she give up her dream of having children to be with Liam? Was her love strong enough never to have any regrets?

Madison rose. "I'm ready to go home, but I can't promise you to give him a chance."

"Okay. I'm here if you need to talk, but so is your uncle."

Madison stiffened. "Katie thinks he's her daddy. He isn't. He's only our uncle." Without waiting for Sarah, Madison entered the house and hurried for the front door.

Sarah followed, pausing briefly in the living room entrance. "Mom, I'm walking Madison home."

"When you get back, maybe you should tell me what's going on." Her mother returned her attention to the book she was reading.

Oh, joy. But, like Madison, she needed to talk to her mom. She'd seen Sarah was upset when she'd charged into the house after going to the park.

Sarah rushed to catch up with Madison. They covered the block and a half in silence. When Madison reached her home, she ignored Liam sitting on the porch swing and went straight inside.

Sarah debated whether to turn around and leave without saying anything to Liam. But she should tell him what she and Madison had talked about. She mounted the steps to the porch, but instead of sitting next to him, she leaned against the railing nearby. Even this close to him, she was torn. She loved him. But was it enough?

"I didn't want her to overhear me telling Katie. I made a mess of this whole situation."

She couldn't see his face clearly because the outside light didn't reach to the far end of the porch, but the weariness in his voice made it clear what he was feeling. "I'm not sure telling her straight out would have been any better. Hopefully she'll come around in time, but as I'm sure you know, she doesn't want you to move."

"What would you have done under my circumstances?"

"Five years ago I left Buffalo, but it didn't erase my pain, and in some ways it delayed it. Our situation is different, though."

He pushed to his feet and closed the space between them. "Could you marry me knowing I could never father a child?"

"Honestly, I don't know. When my daughter died, my dreams of family were snatched away. It left a void in my life."

"I won't be responsible for taking the possibility away from you. I love you too much to do that."

When he said those words, Sarah wanted to pull him into her arms and never let him go. But he pivoted and strode to his front door. "Thank you for taking care of Madison."

His parting words released a dam on her emotions. Tears blurred her vision and streamed down her face. She couldn't wipe them away fast enough.

Quickly she ran for home. *Why, God, did You send me a great man to love who can't have children?*

Pulling weeds in the yard was the perfect task for Sarah on her day off. A light breeze cooled the warm day and in the shade of her oak tree she was comfortable even though the temperature would be in the low nineties by midafternoon. Yesterday at church, Betty had brought the girls with her. Liam hadn't come. According to his aunt, he was working non-stop to put the house on the market by the first week in June.

She only saw him now at the fund-raiser meetings and at swimming class. She missed him more than she realized she would.

Standing on the deck, Gabe barked—again and again.

What was wrong with him? He moved to the back door and continued yelping. She rose.

Nana and Mom were inside. Did he want to go in?

As she strolled toward her black Lab, the scent of smoke teased her nostrils. Another grass fire? She glanced around then began to hurry toward the house. Through the large kitchen window she glimpsed a gray haze.

"Stay," she said to Gabe then felt the door to make sure it wasn't hot.

When she opened it, a rush of heat blasted her in the face. In the kitchen, Nana held a glass of water while flames shot up from a skillet on a burner.

"Don't, Nana," Sarah shouted at the same time her grandmother tossed the water on the fire.

Instantly the flames multiplied and expanded twofold. The alarm in the hall sounded as Sarah raced across the room and tugged on Nana, who was staring at the stove as though paralyzed.

"Nana, we're getting out of here."

The smoke filling the kitchen irritated Sarah's throat and stung her eyes. She practically dragged her grandmother from the house. When she jostled Nana out the door, Sarah spied her purse on the counter not far away. Her cell phone was inside.

"Get away from the house with Gabe."

Sarah hastened to her bag and snatched it off the granite top.

As she ran from the house, Sarah dug into her purse, grabbed her phone and punched in 9-1-1.

After reporting the fire, she hurried Nana out of the backyard. "Where's Mom?"

"Living room the last I saw. Sleeping."

Sarah rounded the front of the house, expecting to see her mother outside because of the alarm going off. She heard the siren in the distance. Help would be here soon, but what if her mother was trapped or smoke had overcome her?

"Stay here, Nana. The fire department is on its way. I need to borrow this dish towel." She removed it from her grandmother's hand that still clutched it.

Wrapping the towel around her face, Sarah rushed to the porch and peered into the front window. Smoke billowed from the kitchen and poured into the connected dining and living rooms. Through the haze, her mother lay on the floor. Not moving.

Sarah fumbled in her purse for the house key and turned the lock to open the door. As she charged into the burning house, the sound of the sirens drew nearer. She grabbed hold of her mother's arms and tugged her toward the entry hall.

A firefighter dashed inside, followed by two others.

"Get them out of here," Liam said to the others behind him. "I'll go after Nana."

Over the noise of the crackling fire, Sarah yelled, "Nana is out front."

Liam disappeared into the hallway.

Maybe he didn't hear her. She started to go after him. Brandon got in front of her and blocked her. "Get out."

"But—"

"We saw your grandmother going in the front door when we pulled up." He moved her toward the front door.

Junior! He was in Nana's bedroom. Sarah hadn't even thought about that. "She's going to her bedroom to get her cat. It's the first one along the back of the house."

"Leave." Brandon pivoted and hurried toward the hallway.

Near the paramedics who were working on her mother, Sarah faced her home, flames now shooting up into the sky and consuming the structure. Nana's bedroom was the closest one to the kitchen. Heartbeat thundering in her ears, Sarah waved off one of the EMTs. Her throat burned and her eyes watered, but she wouldn't move from this spot until she saw Nana, Liam and Brandon come outside.

Smoke snaking through the house, Liam felt his way down the hall, found a door on the left and pushed it open. He searched it before ruling it out. Across from that door was another one. He shoved inside and found Nana holding Junior while she sat on the floor by the window.

"Nana, I'm Liam." He helped her up and tried to raise the bottom pane. It wouldn't budge.

"I couldn't leave him in here." Coughs racked her.

Liam shared his oxygen mask with her then took his ax to break the glass. The door crashed open as Brandon came into the room and grabbed Nana to move her out the way. Liam swung the ax and shattered the window.

"The fire is spreading rapidly in the attic." Brandon, supporting Nana, moved toward Liam.

He poked his head out and quickly assessed their escape route. Eight feet to the sloping ground. "You go out first," he said to Brandon, "and I'll lower her down until you have a good hold on her." Liam took Junior and gave the kitten to Brandon.

His friend leaped to the grass, rolling when he landed with Junior. He put the kitten on the ground and then hurried to the window. "Ready. Hurry. The whole right side is in flames."

"Nana, you have to do as I say. I'm going to pick you up and hand you off to my friend. Understand?"

She nodded.

Thankfully Sarah's grandmother was petite and only weighed about a hundred pounds. Liam wrapped his arms around her middle and guided her legs out the opening first. Nana flailed as she hung on to the side of the house for a few seconds.

Liam poured all his strength into holding on to her. "You're okay, Nana."

Finally, Brandon grabbed her legs and Liam lowered her farther toward the ground.

"I got her," Brandon shouted.

Liam let go and prepared to jump as soon as they were out of the way. As Brandon moved Nana back, an explosion rocked the house, knocking Liam to the side, his shoulder ramming into the floor.

Chapter Thirteen

Numb, Sarah sat with Betty, Madison and Katie in the ER waiting room.

She shouldn't have gone out in the backyard and pulled weeds. She shouldn't have left Nana alone out front. But then her mother might have been caught in the fire. She shouldn't have rescued the litter of kittens, then Nana wouldn't have gone back into the house for Junior.

Now three people she loved were in the hospital. Nana and Mom were heading upstairs. Her mother had a concussion from leaping off the couch when the alarm went off. She'd slipped and hit the coffee table, but the doctor said she should be better in a few days; her overnight stay merely a precaution. Nana had broken her hip from the force of the hot water heater exploding; she'd fallen back into Brandon. Her grandmother would be in the hospital for a while then, probably a rehab facility. Sarah needed to go up to see them, but she couldn't leave until she knew Liam would live. A piece of the bedroom ceiling had trapped him, but Brandon and the firefighters had managed to get the fire under control well enough to get Liam out.

She had her arms around both girls. They leaned against her, not saying a word as the minutes ticked away. Betty sat across from them as though in shock, and Sarah understood that feeling. So much had happened in a brief time, the least being the destruction of her childhood home.

Finally, Brandon came to the doorway and motioned for her to come to him.

"I'll be right back. I'm going to get something to drink. Do you want anything?"

Betty shook her head while Madison and Katie murmured, "No."

She met Brandon outside in the hallway. "What's going on?"

"The doctor will be here shortly to talk with Betty, but they're taking Liam to a room. Like your mother, he has a concussion but also several cracked ribs and smoke inhalation."

"I'm staying. I won't leave until I've seen that Liam is all right."

"I figured that. They're going to let you take

the girls into the room so they can see he's alive. Betty, too. On the ambulance ride to the hospital, Liam rallied for a few minutes. He wants you to take care of his nieces. He's afraid it'll be too much for his aunt."

"I'll do anything I can." She'd walked away from the car wreck alive while Peter and her daughter had died. And now she'd survived another tragedy. This time she wasn't going to blame herself. The fire was an unfortunate accident. Putting blame on someone wouldn't make the pain go away.

Half an hour later Sarah, Betty and the girls left Nana's room after visiting Sarah's mother. Now they headed for Liam's room.

Brandon was inside and stood when they entered. "He was given something for the pain and is sleeping. Sorry, I thought he'd still be awake."

"Rest is the best thing for him. Right, Madison, Katie?"

"When will we be able to talk to him?" Madison asked in such a low tone Sarah barely heard her over Katie's sobs.

Betty walked to the bed and kissed Liam on the forehead. His girls did the same thing.

When Sarah approached Liam, the fast beating of her heart drowned out the beeping sounds from the machine. Her attention focused only on one thing: Liam hooked up to monitors, his face pale, his eyes closed, his long lashes sweeping the tops of his cheeks.

She leaned close and whispered, "I love you," then took his free hand and kissed the palm. When she swung around, she swallowed the tears threatening. His nieces didn't need to see them. "We'll come back tomorrow morning to visit your uncle. You'll see. He'll be much better then."

"What about school?" Madison asked, her gaze never leaving her uncle's face.

"I think you can miss one day under the circumstances, but you'll need to go on Wednesday. Your uncle wants me to watch you both." Sarah had already mentioned that to Betty, who had been relieved. "But I don't have a place to stay."

The girls ran to her and enveloped her in a hug.

Madison looked up and said, "You can stay at our house anytime."

Later that night Sarah dropped Betty off at her home. Brandon had taken her by the fire station to pick up Liam's vehicle, since Sarah's and her mother's car had been totaled when the ceiling fell in on them in the garage. One of many things that would have to be replaced, but she wasn't going to think about her problems. The one thing she could do for Liam was take good care of his nieces as if they were her daughters.

Sarah entered Katie's bedroom to say goodnight to her. Hugging Blackie against her, the little girl fought to keep her eyes open.

She climbed into bed. "I want to pray."

Sarah sat next to Katie, folded her hands together and bowed her head.

"God, take care of my daddy in Heaven and my daddy in the hospital. Amen." She wiggled under the covers with Blackie still in her arms. The kitten didn't seem to mind the attention at all.

"Good night, sweetie." Sarah kissed Katie's forehead and started to leave.

"Sarah, I love you. I'm glad you're here."

When Sarah left, shutting the door, she leaned against the wall between the girls' rooms. Closing her eyes, she relished the words Katie had said. Her heart seemed close to bursting. She imagined Emma, who would have been near Katie's age, saying those words to her. For a few moments she experienced what it felt like to be a mother and loved by a child.

Straightening, Sarah continued into Madison's room. She had been quiet most of the evening since they'd come home. The girl sat on the edge of the bed while Buffy rubbed herself against Madison's legs. Sarah cleared her throat and the child lifted her head, worry and sadness reflected in her gaze.

"He'll be all right, won't he?" Her blue eyes glistened.

"Of course. The doctor said so, and I know it in here." Sarah placed her hand over her heart.

"I'm not mad anymore at Katie for calling him Daddy. He's like a father. I don't want anything to happen to him. I've already lost one dad. I don't want to lose another."

The child's words were exactly what Sarah felt, except it wasn't a dad but a husband. She'd already lost one and she didn't want to lose Liam. She wanted him to stay. Somehow she had to make him see that.

Sarah covered Madison's hand. "Time for bed. Or we'll be so tired when we go to see your uncle tomorrow, we won't be able to keep our eyes open."

The girl rose and climbed into bed. She stopped, twisted back to Sarah and embraced her. "I'm glad you're here."

Hours later, staring up at the ceiling in the spare bedroom, Sarah came to a decision, and she intended to let Liam know.

On Wednesday, after visiting her grand-mother in the hospital, Sarah hurried to Liam's room. She should have some alone time with him. The girls had gone to school today, and she'd had Brandon make sure no off-duty fire-fighter came to visit Liam. If Brandon had to camp out at the elevator, he would to give her what she wanted.

At the door to Liam's room, she waved to Brandon then headed inside.

Liam's gaze shifted to her. "I thought you'd be at work, especially since your mother is tak-ing some time off."

"I've rearranged a few appointments. Every-one, even Beatrice, has been understanding. Mom intends to go back to work on Friday, but at least she's listening to the doctor and tak-ing a few days off. I'll be heading to work in a while. I just dropped the girls off at school, and I promised I would bring them back this afternoon."

"I should be leaving the hospital tomorrow, but I won't be able to work for a couple of weeks. The doctor will have to clear me before the captain will let me go back." He adjusted the bed so he sat up higher. "How are Madi-son and Katie doing?"

"Great. Since they have been able to visit you, they aren't as worried as they were at first. Have you been getting enough rest?"

"Are you kidding? There has been a steady stream of people through here. I'll rest when I get home. Did your mother take me up on staying at my house?"

"Only until you come home. Later we're going to look for a furnished apartment. I'll take the girls with us. They think we're going on an adventure. They want us to rent an apartment with a pool."

He chuckled then winced. "Don't make me laugh. It hurts."

"I won't stay long, but I wanted to talk to you alone before I went into work."

"Why?" he asked in a wary tone.

"A couple of weeks ago you had your say, and now I'm going to have mine. I love you, Liam McGregory. That isn't going to change, so how in the world would I ever marry anyone else and have that baby you think I want more than you?"

He blinked and looked away. "I'm sure you believe that now. But in five or ten years, you'll regret not having children, and then you'll begin to resent me. I can't go through another marriage like that."

"How long did it take your ex-wife to feel that way?"

He frowned. "A year after we got a second opinion about my condition."

"Well, for your information, I'm not her. I don't want you to leave. I want us to be together."

"No." He stared out the window. "I think you should go."

She wanted to argue with him but instead decided to leave for the time being. At the door she glanced back at him watching her. "I need you to know, I love you and I love your nieces as if they were my own children."

Then she left. She wouldn't beg, but she would make him realize he was wrong about her.

At the bachelor auction, Sarah sat at the front table nearest the stage between Pastor Collins and Brandon, who had returned to his seat after being bachelor number fifteen. Now it was Liam's turn. She'd been waiting all night for this moment.

Ever since he'd left the hospital, Liam had avoided her. Other than a quick glance at church last Sunday, she hadn't seen him. Colt had brought the girls to the pool for their swimming lessons. She had no intention of letting their last time alone be their conversation in his hospital room.

"Liam McGregory is our last bachelor tonight. Recently injured while saving a woman from a burning house, he is dedicated to his job and his family. Let's end the evening with a bang. We've already brought in more money for the summer day camp than any other fundraiser in the past. Liam is offering to cook dinner for his date on a day of her choice."

As Liam walked onto the stage, his cheeks were red. He looked dynamite in his tuxedo, but his blush told Sarah what he thought of his introduction by the mayor's wife. As he strolled slowly across the stage the crowd went wild, clapping and cheering.

The auctioneer stepped up to the podium and opened the bidding with fifty dollars. Woman after woman stood and placed a bid. As it slowed down Sarah finally made her first one.

Britney held up her hand and upped the price by ten dollars.

Sarah felt everyone's gaze on her as she rose. This was for charity. "Six hundred dollars."

Silence filled the large hall.

"Going once. Twice. Sold to this pretty little lady for six hundred dollars." The auctioneer pointed his gavel at Sarah.

She headed for the back of the room to pay for her date with the man she loved. It was worth every penny. He had to go out with her whether he wanted to or not.

After she wrote her check, she turned to leave and ran right into Liam. He steadied her then took her hand and tugged her out the door into the church hallway.

He swiveled toward her. "What are you doing?"

"Getting a date with you since you've been avoiding me. I get to pick the day for our date, right?"

Frowning, he nodded.

"I pick tonight. Right now."

"It's after ten."

"That's okay. What I have to say won't take that long. Let's go."

"What? Where?"

"The park. I'm driving." She pulled her keys to her rental car out of her pocket.

"You had this all planned?"

"Yes. I don't give up easily."

"What about Madison and Katie?"

"Betty and Mom are taking care of them."

"I feel a little ridiculous going to the park in a tuxedo."

"Well, I'm not exactly dressed for the park, either. Most women don't wear cocktail dresses and three-inch high heels there."

Sarah pulled into the parking lot nearest the bench where he'd first told her about leaving Buffalo. She shifted toward him, the light from the parking lot illuminating the area. "Will you come with me?"

"Do I have a choice?"

"Yes. Always."

He opened the door and slid out carefully, being mindful of his healing ribs.

Sarah sighed. *Lord, I need help convincing him I'm the best for him. Please help me to know what to say.*

She climbed from the rental car and headed toward the bench silhouetted in the light from the security lamp. Liam had already taken a seat. He gazed at her as she walked toward him in high heels on the soft grass. She sat next to him, and everything she'd planned to say to him fled her mind.

"I've never been kidnapped before," he finally said, breaking the long silence.

"And you still haven't been. I bought you fair and square."

Liam grinned. "So what do you want to tell me?"

"That you're a coward."

"Wow, that was blunt. Wasn't I the one who saved your grandmother?"

"For that I will always be grateful. No, you're a coward when it comes to your emotions. You tell me you love me, but we can't be together because I *might* in the future leave you because of something your ex-wife did. Do you think so little of me? Of yourself?

"You have so much more to offer than your ability to father children. You've forged a family out of a difficult situation. You've run into burning buildings to rescue someone in jeopardy. You moved here to give your nieces a better chance to bond with you. You were thrown into fatherhood suddenly with no preparation. And you're only wanting to leave in August because you're afraid of what we have."

"I'm not afraid to love. I'm afraid of losing love."

She took both his hands in hers. "So am I. We've both gone through it under different circumstances, but that should also make us realize how precious love is and want to hold on to it even more."

"From the beginning I've known you would be a great mother. Then when I heard the pain in your voice when you were talking about how close you came to being a mother and it was snatched away, I knew I couldn't stand in your way of having that."

"But you are. I believe we were brought together for a reason. You just happened to find my dog. I just happened to find your poster on the pole where I usually don't go. I'm meant to be a mother to Madison and Katie. I *want* to be. I love them. I've discovered how much, taking care of them while you were in the hospital." She squeezed his hands gently. "*You* are the man I love and want to spend the rest of my life with."

"But what if—"

She covered his mouth with her fingers. "Do you love me?"

"Yes."

"Then there are no what-ifs. Life is a risk, but the Lord tells us not to spend our time worrying about the future. A waste of time because we don't know what the future will be. He wants us to give our worry to Him. He'll take care of it. That's how I want to live."

He lifted her hand and kissed it. "I may need some help with that."

"We'll help each other."

Liam wrapped his arms around her and pulled her against him, settling his mouth on hers. "I love you, Sarah. It should be an interesting journey with you."

Epilogue

New Year's Eve

In a cream-colored gown, Sarah held Katie's hand and walked down the center aisle at Buffalo Community Church toward Liam with Madison in pink taffeta standing next to him. At the altar, Katie, in a similar dress as her sister but purple, stood on her tiptoes and kissed Sarah's cheek then took her place next to Sarah.

Their wedding was a little unusual, but they had wanted to get married with the girls standing up for them. It had started out small, but Mom, Betty and Nana had turned it into a huge production with most of the members of the church in attendance, all the firefighters and other friends and family, even some of Liam's from Dallas.

When Pastor Collins announced to the large

audience that they were husband and wife, Liam took Sarah into his arms and kissed her as though he'd claimed her forever. From the beginning she'd given her heart to Liam and hadn't regretted it one moment. Already she felt as though she were part of his family.

After taking Katie's hand, Liam clasped Sarah's, and she held Madison's. Together, as a family, the four made their way down the aisle while the guests clapped. Out in the lobby, the guests engulfed them in well wishes as the doors to the reception hall were opened.

As Sarah moved into the cavernous room, memories of that June night after the bachelor auction overwhelmed her. Now her dream had come full circle. She'd gained a husband and two adorable daughters.

"I love the idea we're starting a brand-new year as husband and wife," Liam whispered as they made their way toward the table where the four-tier wedding cake sat, decorated in white frosting with pink and purple flowers.

"Mom and Nana outdid themselves with that."

"Madison and Katie are both going to be master chefs between me and your mom and Nana."

"On holidays we might have too many cooks in the kitchen."

At the table Liam faced her, his golden-brown eyes twinkling. "And you'll be outside in the garden with our pets."

She touched Liam's cheek. "You're always welcome to join me."

He dipped his head toward hers, about to kiss her, when Aunt Betty presented them with a silver knife to cut the cake. "Okay, you two, there's plenty of time for that on your honeymoon. You've got some hungry guests."

Sarah laughed. "Look who's most eager?"

Beaming, Madison and Katie stood next to the table with their plates in their hands.

"And right behind them is Nana." Liam stepped toward the cake with the silver knife.

Sarah covered his hand on the hilt. "Our first task together as a married couple."

"But not our last."

They pressed the blade into the wedding cake, cutting the first piece. A round of applause from the guests echoed through the reception hall.

Liam captured her gaze. "I guess I'll be drummed out of the Single Dads' Club now, but that's okay. I have what I want the most."

Then he kissed her.

* * * * *

Dear Reader,

This book is the start of a new series about single dads and the support group that they attend. Support groups are a wonderful way to help people cope with difficult or unfamiliar situations.

At times, we have all needed support. And we often turn to God, family and friends. But what if those people we usually seek support from haven't gone what we're going through? That's why support groups can be so important. The Lord wants us to band together to help each other. Going through a problem without support can sometimes overwhelm a person. Many communities and churches have created support groups for this very reason. If there isn't one where you live, why not start one? You might be surprised how many others are going through the same thing.

I love hearing from readers. You can contact me at margaretdaley@gmail.com or at P.O. Box 2074, Tulsa, OK 74101. You can also learn more about my books at http://www.margaretdaley. com. I have a newsletter that you can sign up for on my website.

Best wishes,

Margaret Daley

REQUEST YOUR FREE BOOKS!
2 FREE WHOLESOME ROMANCE NOVELS IN LARGER PRINT
PLUS 2 FREE MYSTERY GIFTS

✼✼✼✼✼✼✼✼✼✼✼✼✼✼✼✼✼✼✼✼✼✼✼✼

HEARTWARMING™

✼✼✼✼✼✼✼✼✼✼✼✼✼✼✼✼✼✼✼✼✼✼✼✼

Wholesome, tender romances

YES! Please send me 2 FREE Harlequin® Heartwarming Larger-Print novels and my 2 FREE mystery gifts (gifts worth about $10). After receiving them, if I don't wish to receive any more books, I can return the shipping statement marked "cancel." If I don't cancel, I will receive 4 brand-new larger-print novels every month and be billed just $5.24 per book in the U.S. or $5.99 per book in Canada. That's a savings of at least 19% off the cover price. It's quite a bargain! Shipping and handling is just 50¢ per book in the U.S. and 75¢ per book in Canada.* I understand that accepting the 2 free books and gifts places me under no obligation to buy anything. I can always return a shipment and cancel at any time. Even if I never buy another book, the two free books and gifts are mine to keep forever.

161/361 IDN GHX2

Name _____ (PLEASE PRINT) _____

Address _____ Apt. # _____

City _____ State/Prov. _____ Zip/Postal Code _____

Signature (if under 18, a parent or guardian must sign) _____

Mail to the **Reader Service**:
IN U.S.A.: P.O. Box 1867, Buffalo, NY 14240-1867
IN CANADA: P.O. Box 609, Fort Erie, Ontario L2A 5X3

* Terms and prices subject to change without notice. Prices do not include applicable taxes. Sales tax applicable in N.Y. Canadian residents will be charged applicable taxes. Offer not valid in Quebec. This offer is limited to one order per household. Not valid for current subscribers to Harlequin Heartwarming larger-print books. All orders subject to credit approval. Credit or debit balances in a customer's account(s) may be offset by any other outstanding balance owed by or to the customer. Please allow 4 to 6 weeks for delivery. Offer available while quantities last.

Your Privacy—The Reader Service is committed to protecting your privacy. Our Privacy Policy is available online at www.ReaderService.com or upon request from the Reader Service.

We make a portion of our mailing list available to reputable third parties that offer products we believe may interest you. If you prefer that we not exchange your name with third parties, or if you wish to clarify or modify your communication preferences, please visit us at www.ReaderService.com/consumerchoice or write to us at Reader Service Preference Service, P.O. Box 9062, Buffalo, NY 14240-9062. Include your complete name and address.

HW15

YES! Please send me **The Montana Mavericks Collection** in Larger Print. This collection begins with 3 FREE books and 2 FREE gifts (gifts valued at approx. $20.00 retail) in the first shipment, along with the other first 4 books from the collection! If I do not cancel, I will receive 8 monthly shipments until I have the entire 51-book Montana Mavericks collection. I will receive 2 or 3 FREE books in each shipment and I will pay just $4.99 US/ $5.89 CDN for each of the other four books in each shipment, plus $2.99 for shipping and handling per shipment.*If I decide to keep the entire collection, I'll have paid for only 32 books, because 19 books are FREE! I understand that accepting the 3 free books and gifts places me under no obligation to buy anything. I can always return a shipment and cancel at any time. My free books and gifts are mine to keep no matter what I decide.

263 HCN 2404   463 HCN 2404

Name _____ (PLEASE PRINT) _____

Address _____ Apt. # _____

City _____ State/Prov. _____ Zip/Postal Code _____

Signature (if under 18, a parent or guardian must sign)

Mail to the **Reader Service:**

IN U.S.A.: P.O. Box 1867, Buffalo, NY 14240-1867
IN CANADA: P.O. Box 609, Fort Erie, Ontario L2A 5X3

MMLPBPA15